NEW YORK REVIEW BOOKS
CLASSICS

THE MAN WHO
WATCHED TRAINS GO BY

GEORGES SIMENON (1903–1989) was born in Liège, Belgium. He went to work as a reporter at the age of fifteen and in 1923 moved to Paris, where under various pseudonyms he became a highly successful and prolific author of pulp fiction while leading a dazzling social life. In the early 1930s, Simenon emerged as a writer under his own name, gaining renown for his detective stories featuring Inspector Maigret. He also began to write his psychological novels, or *romans durs*—books in which he displays a sympathetic awareness of the emotional and spiritual pain underlying the routines of daily life. Having written nearly two hundred books under his own name and become the best-selling author in the world, Simenon retired as a novelist in 1973, devoting himself instead to dictating memoirs that filled thousands of pages.

LUC SANTE teaches writing and the history of photography at Bard College. His books include *Low Life*, *Evidence*, and *The Factory of Facts*.

OTHER BOOKS BY GEORGES SIMENON
PUBLISHED BY NYRB CLASSICS

Dirty Snow
Monsieur Monde Vanishes
Three Bedrooms in Manhattan
Tropic Moon

THE MAN WHO WATCHED TRAINS GO BY

GEORGES SIMENON

A new translation by

MARC ROMANO

D. THIN

Introduction by

LUC SANTE

NEW YORK REVIEW BOOKS

New York

THIS IS A NEW YORK REVIEW BOOK
PUBLISHED BY THE NEW YORK REVIEW OF BOOKS
1755 Broadway, New York, NY 10019
www.nyrb.com

Library of Congress Cataloging-in-Publication Data
Simenon, Georges, 1903–
  [Homme qui regardait passer les trains.]
  The man who watched trains go by / by Georges Simenon ; introduction by Luc Sante ;
translated by Marc Romano.
     p. cm. — (New York Review Books classics)
  ISBN 1-59017-149-7 (alk. paper)
  I. Romano, Marc. II. Title. III. Series.
  PQ2637.I53H6213 2005
  843'.912—dc22
                              2005008102

ISBN: 978-1-59017-149-3

Printed in the United States of America on acid-free paper.
10 9 8 7 6 5 4 3 2

INTRODUCTION

THE LEGEND of Georges Simenon expresses itself in statistics: four hundred books, ten thousand women, half a million pencils, some exalted quantity of pipes. The books have gone through staggering numbers of editions, been translated into every possible language, made into some sixty movies and innumerable items for television. The Simenon legend is industrial, like one of those nineteenth-century literary factories, of which Balzac and Dumas come most readily to mind. Unlike Dumas, however, Simenon could never be accused of running an atelier in which underlings came up with plots and undertook the less glamorous portions of the labor. He may have relied upon typists and secretaries, some of them cleverly disguised as wives, but every word he wrote originated in the fevered recesses of his own mind.

The first thing I ever knew about Simenon was that he had written an entire novel while enclosed in a glass booth, in full view of the public. I heard this from my father, and for some reason I was persuaded that he himself had witnessed the stunt, which did not seem implausible since our town was only ten or fifteen miles from Simenon's native city of Liège, in southern Belgium. But the feat never actually occurred, although a Parisian publicist nearly talked Simenon into pulling it off in the mid-1930s, and my father was not the only person who believed it had really happened. By that point Simenon was publishing from three to twelve books a year, which must have seemed leisurely to him after the frantic pace of his first professional decade; in 1929 he had achieved his peak of annual production: forty books, under an assortment of pseudonyms.

Perhaps because he wished to dispel the notion that he employed subcontractors, Simenon allowed his method to be known. On the other hand, maybe he told interviewers about it just because the method itself was so prodigious. On a large yellow envelope he would, over the course of a week or two, write the names of his characters and whatever else he knew about their lives and backgrounds: their ages, where they had gone to school, their parents' professions. The envelope might additionally contain street maps of the novel's setting, although it would never say a word about the book's eventual plot. Once he was satisfied with these notes he would enter the hermitage of his study and knock off the book at the rate of a chapter every morning, optimally in a week or ten days. After finishing he would be drained, battered by violent psychological storms and concurrent physical symptoms. It was a bit as if he had given birth. It should be noted that he could write books this way even when he was ostensibly on vacation.

Not all of his books were written so quickly, although the majority of them were. In this and many other countries, Simenon is best known for his detective novels, featuring the agreeable, implacable, slow-moving, intuitive, preternaturally observant Inspector Maigret. But among the novels he published under his own name, the Maigret books are outnumbered nearly two to one by the titles he called *romans durs*, "hard novels," hard in the sense that they are uncomfortable. In nearly all of these books a character, generally someone who has been leading a humdrum, predictable existence, is confronted by an unexpected occurrence, setting in motion a series of events that will test his limits, an experience he may not survive. These books feature a broad range of characters, in a diverse collection of settings, who are subjected to an apparently unlimited inventory of psychological torments. You imagine Simenon selecting a pedestrian seen in passing somewhere near one of his homes or on one of his many travels, speculating as to what that person's internal and external life must be like, and then devising a suitable chamber of horrors in which to release his captive specimen.

Because Simenon was so prolific and so various it is difficult to render a concise account of his work, and impossible to cite any one book as typical of him. His early, pseudonymous output is pretty crude—after reading one or two of the books signed "Georges Sim" or "Gom Gut" you cease marveling that he was able to produce so many so quickly—and several of the earliest Maigrets feature plot turns that would not seem out of place in a Philo Vance mystery, but even then, in the early 1930s, he was capable of writing emotionally demanding novels that drive the knife deep into the reader's heart. Simenon, the son of first-generation petit-bourgeois parents who took in lodgers to supplement the family income and whose idea of higher education was limited to secondary school with the Christian Brothers, entered his literary career with a distinctly working-class idea of the trade. It was a means of living by one's wits, related to show biz and not too far from simple hustling, and it required a constant output, with no pretensions and no looking back. Somewhere along the line, though, he made his signal discovery, that so much of what passes for literature merely consists of studies of people in their clothing, that is, people operating within the rigid confines of social codes. He, on the other hand, wanted to write about the naked human, who is forced by circumstances to confront life without the usual protections.

Those same social codes made him an outsider and kept him one even at the height of his fame. He had served his

apprenticeship writing pulp fiction and had cemented his reputation with detective novels; furthermore he was Belgian. He
also lacked a writing style detectable by the belletristic appara-
tus of the pre-war era. Therefore he was forever barred from
being accepted as a man of letters by the people in Paris who
decided such things, for all that André Gide was his great ad-
mirer and sponsor and that he enjoyed friendships with the
likes of Jean Cocteau and Henry Miller. At first he chafed at
this restriction, the first symptom of his discontent being that
he packed Inspector Maigret off to rural retirement in 1934—
although he bowed to popular demand and brought him back
eight years later, and spent the last quarter-century of his career
alternating metronomically between the Maigrets and the "hard
novels," which he also called *roman-romans*, "novel-novels."
The latter are so numerous—there are 117 of them—that I con-
fess to not having read even half, but they include many that
should be much better known than they are. Simenon's work,
when you begin to delve into it, is unlike that of any other author except perhaps Balzac—it seems less like the labor of one
person than an entire, hitherto unsuspected national literature,
not just in its size but in the range of its approaches and pre-
occupations. Simenon may be, finally, the most famous un-
known writer of the twentieth century.

———

The Man Who Watched Trains Go By was published in 1938,
Simenon's eleventh novel that year. It tells the story of Kees
Popinga, chief clerk of a ships' chandlery in the northern Dutch
city of Groningen, a man satisfied that his life is the best one
possible in the best of all possible worlds. (Simenon often de-
picted Dutch and Flemish characters as possessing that sort of

buttoned-up smugness.) His bicycle is the finest one obtainable, his family patronizes the city's best grocery and buys only the highest-quality goods, his daily routine runs like clockwork and is a source of deep satisfaction. Then it all blows up in his face. His employer, Julius de Coster the Younger, an irreproachable bourgeois, turns out to have been cooking the books, ruining the business, and as the novel starts is on the point of fleeing the country, having faked his own suicide.

Whatever pin was holding Popinga together has been pulled out. First he refuses to get up in the morning, alarming his family, who do not yet know what has happened. Then he resolves to pay a call on de Coster's mistress, whom he now decides he deserves just as much as his erstwhile boss, but his approach is so awkward that he kills her, more or less unintentionally. He flees to Paris, and when he learns that he is wanted for murder he begins to fancy himself a criminal mastermind. He engages in what he conceives of as a cat-and-mouse game with the Parisian police, all the while writing taunting letters to the press. The further he sinks into abjection the more megalomaniacal he becomes. He resembles an automobile in a cartoon, the driver continuing to propel it forward as it loses first its roof, then its doors, hood, tires, engine, until it is finally just a board rolling on its axles. Popinga is also a bit like Flitcraft, the protagonist of the story that Sam Spade tells Brigid O'Shaughnessy in Dashiell Hammett's *The Maltese Falcon*. Passing by a construction site, Flitcraft is narrowly missed by a falling beam. He is shaken to his roots. "He felt like somebody had taken the lid off life and let him look at the works." He is so unmoored that he walks out of his life altogether, leaving behind wife, children, home, business, and money. When Spade catches up with him, though, he is living in a city not far away, remarried, with a new baby and a successful business. Unlike

Popinga, "he adjusted to beams falling, and then no more of them fell, and he adjusted himself to them not falling."*

Simenon read psychology texts for fun (he was especially fond of the works of Alfred Adler), and it is no accident that his novels can sometimes sound, in summary, like clinical case studies. He knows enough about humans, though, that his subjects can never be reduced to the sum of their defects. Here he takes several knowing pokes at the whole idea of psychological evaluation, among them by having an eminent specialist diagnose Popinga long-distance for the benefit of the newspapers—he is paranoid, the great man decides, but then he quickly disavows his own diagnosis. Popinga, who has not up to then seemed especially paranoid, promptly begins imagining police spies everywhere. He is a megalomaniac, but as it were on a reduced scale. He is such a criminal mastermind that he gets fleeced by a real criminal, and nearly gets shot when he briefly and unwittingly becomes the third leg of a romantic triangle. He hates women, but does far more harm to the ones he desires than the ones he actually wishes to hurt. He makes himself most glaringly visible when he decides to vanish altogether. The collapse of his world, as heralded by the fall of the house of de Coster, prompts him to take dramatic, proto-existential action, but everything he does from that moment on results in failure —except chess, at which he is brilliant. He is, finally, incapable

---

*Although Simenon knew and liked Hammett's work—the admiration was mutual—there is no real reason to think that Flitcraft's story inspired Popinga's, especially since Popinga is not the only one of Simenon's protagonists who walks out on his life, or whose life unravels all at once. But there is an eerie resemblance between Julius de Coster, having suddenly shucked off respectability, getting drunk in a dive, and talking like an experienced con artist, and the boss in Jean Renoir's great Popular Front fable *Le Crime de M. Lange* (1936). When the publisher Batala (brilliantly played by Jules Berry), who has absconded in a fashion nearly identical to de Coster, comes back dressed as a priest to tease and threaten his former employee Lange, he suddenly sounds like an underworld veteran. Renoir was the first to adapt Simenon for the screen, with *La Nuit du carrefour* (1932), and the two remained friendly.

of filling any role other than the one he inhabited at the beginning of the story. *The Man Who Watched Trains Go By* is a galling book. You the reader assume the fears and tribulations of a character you cannot possibly like. You live and die (so to speak), sweat and cringe with him. You carry a knot in your chest as he drags himself around ever bleaker and more remote corners of Paris. You become almost physically uncomfortable on his behalf, even as you are repulsed by him. And then, after you have closed the book and put it back on the shelf, you realize that all along you have been reading a comedy.

—Luc Sante

THE MAN WHO WATCHED
TRAINS GO BY

I

In which Julius de Coster the Younger gets drunk at the Little Saint-George, and the impossible suddenly breaches the dykes of everyday life.

As FAR as Kees Popinga was personally concerned, it should be admitted that at eight in the evening there was still time: his fate, among others, had yet to be sealed. But time for what? And what else could he have done other than what he did do, convinced as he was that his actions were of no more consequence than during the thousands and thousands of days that had gone before?

He would have shrugged in disbelief had someone told him that his life was about to change radically, that the photograph on the side table showing him standing in the middle of his family, with one hand casually resting on the back of a chair, would soon be printed in every newspaper across Europe.

In fact, had he honestly searched within himself for something that presaged the violent future, it is altogether unlikely that he would ever have settled upon the fleeting, almost shameful emotion that he experienced whenever he saw a train going by—especially a night train, with its blinds pulled down over the mystery of the passengers inside.

As to going so far as to tell him to his face that at that very moment his boss, Julius de Coster the Younger, was sitting at a table in the Little Saint-George and systematically getting drunk—that would have been a complete waste of time. Kees Popinga had no patience for nonsense. When it came to people and to things, he had his mind made up.

Yet, unbelievable as it was, Julius de Coster the Younger really and truly was at the Little Saint-George.

And in Amsterdam, in a suite at the Carlton, a certain Pamela was taking a bath before heading out to Tuchinski's, the fashionable nightclub of the moment.

What did that have to do with Popinga? Or that in Paris, at Melie's, a little restaurant on the rue Blanche, there was a certain Jeanne Rozier, a redhead, who was sitting at a table with a man named Louis and serving herself some mustard. "Are you working tonight?" she asked.

And, in Juvisy, not far from the train yard, on Fountainebleau road, a garage mechanic and his sister Rose...

But none of that existed yet. It was part of the future, the immediate future of Kees Popinga, who, on this Wednesday, December 28th, at eight in the evening, hadn't the least suspicion of what lay ahead and was getting ready to smoke a cigar.

———

He would never have admitted it to anyone—it might have been construed as a criticism of family life—but after dinner he had a tendency to nod off. It wasn't the meal itself. Like most Dutch families, they ate a light dinner: tea, buttered bread, cold cuts, slices of cheese, sometimes dessert.

Probably the stove was to blame. It was an imposing stove, the best money could buy, covered in green ceramic tiles and heavily ornamented in nickel, a stove that was no ordinary stove. Its warmth and steady respiration set the pace for the whole house.

The cigar boxes were on the marble mantelpiece, and Popinga was taking his time choosing among them. He sniffed at the tobacco and crackled it, because that was what you did if you wanted to enjoy a cigar. That was the way it was always done.

The table was cleared, and Popinga's fifteen-year-old auburn-haired daughter Frida had spread out her schoolbooks in the lamplight. She contemplated them at length with great dark eyes that were empty of expression—or else unfathomable.

And so things proceeded as usual. Carl, a boy of thirteen, offered his forehead to his mother, then to his father. He kissed his sister and went upstairs to bed.

The stove snored away. Out of habit, Kees asked, "What are you doing, Mother?"

He said "Mother" because of the children.

"Bringing my album up to date."

She was forty years old and as gracious and dignified as the house itself, its people and possessions. You might even have gone so far as to say that she, like the stove, was of the highest quality. A Dutch wife of the highest quality! Kees was always talking about things that were of the highest quality. It was one of his obsessions.

In fact when it came to quality, only their chocolate was second-rate. If they continued to buy the same brand, it was because in every package there was a picture and every one of those pictures had a place appointed for it in a special album that within several years would contain a color reproduction of every flower in the world.

So Mrs. Popinga settled down in front of the aforementioned album to arrange her pictures while Kees fiddled with the knobs on the radio. Soon he had succeeded in drowning out the whole world except for the voice of a soprano and the intermittent clatter of plates from the kitchen, where the maid was cleaning up.

The air was so heavy that the cigar smoke didn't even rise to the ceiling. It lingered instead around Kees's face, where, from time to time, he waved it away like a cobweb.

It had been like this for fifteen years, hadn't it? They were almost frozen in place.

At eight-thirty, however, or just before, when the soprano had fallen silent and a voice was droning out the stock-market results, Kees uncrossed his legs, looked at his cigar, and hesitantly announced, "I wonder if everything really is good to go on board the *Ocean III*."

Silence. The snoring of the stove. Mrs. Popinga had time to paste two more pictures in her album. Frida turned a page of her notebook.

"Perhaps it would be just as well if I went to take a look."

And so the die was cast! There was still time to smoke a quarter-inch of cigar, to stretch, to hear the orchestra tuning up in the Hilversum Auditorium—and then Kees was caught in the net.

From this moment on, each second weighed more heavily than all the seconds he'd lived through before; each of his actions took on as much importance as those of the statesmen whose least gestures were reported in the newspapers.

The maid brought him his big gray overcoat, his fur-lined gloves, and his hat. She slipped galoshes over his shoes while he tamely lifted one foot and then the other.

He kissed his wife and his daughter, noting again that he had no idea what the latter was thinking about and that perhaps it was nothing at all. Then, in the hallway, he couldn't decide whether or not to take his bicycle, a nickel-plated bicycle with gears and about the best you could imagine.

He made up his mind to go on foot, left his house, and turned around with satisfaction. It was practically a villa—he'd designed it and oversaw the construction himself—and even if it wasn't the biggest house in the neighborhood, it was by far the best designed and best looking of the lot.

The neighborhood itself, part of a new development set a bit back from the road to Delfzijl—it was the nicest and cleanest one in all Groningen, wasn't it?

Up till now, Kees Popinga's life had been entirely filled with satisfactions of just this sort. And they were genuine because, after all, it was impossible for anyone to claim that something that was of the highest quality was not of the highest quality, that a well-constructed house wasn't well constructed, or, say, that Oosting's didn't make the best sausage in town.

It was cold—a sharp and bracing cold. His rubber soles crunched on the hardened snow. With his hands in his pockets and his cigar between his lips, Kees walked toward the harbor. He wondered if everything was in fact in order aboard the *Ocean III*.

He hadn't brought up the question simply as an excuse. Not that he was the least bit unhappy to be out walking in the brisk night air instead of dozing off in the stale warmth of his house. But he would never have allowed himself to think, in an official capacity, that there was any place in the world that was sweeter than his own hearth and home. Which is why, whenever he heard a train passing by, he blushed, surprised by a strange, anxious feeling—almost a kind of regret.

No, the *Ocean III* was as real as real could be, and Popinga's nocturnal visit was a professional obligation. At Julius de Coster and Son he functioned both as head manager and as the owner's representative. The company of Julius de Coster and Son was the largest outfitter of ships not only in Groningen but in all of Dutch Frisia. It supplied everything from cordage and fuel oil to coal, not to mention liquor and other provisions.

And the *Ocean III*, which would have to sail at midnight in order to cross the canal ahead of the tide, had placed a large order toward the end of the afternoon.

Kees spotted the ship from a distance: a three-masted clipper. Along the Wilhelmina Canal the docks were deserted, though cluttered here and there with mooring lines. Kees sidestepped them nimbly, then scaled the pilot's ladder like a man who was used to such things. Without hesitating, he headed toward the captain's cabin.

And, strictly speaking, this was the last time that his fate might have been averted. Kees could still have turned around, but he didn't know it. He pushed the door open and found himself face-to-face with a spluttering red-faced giant of a man, who was heaping him with every oath and insult he could think of.

Something altogether unimaginable had happened, at least for those familiar with the reputation of the firm of Julius de Coster and Son: the tanker that had been set to deliver the fuel oil at seven o'clock—and Kees Popinga himself had placed that order—had failed to appear. Not only had the boat not berthed beside the *Ocean III*, but worse, there was no one aboard and the other provisions hadn't been delivered, either.

Five minutes later, a muttering Popinga climbed back down to the dock, swearing that there must have been some misunderstanding and promising to straighten it out.

His cigar had gone out. He was sorry now that he hadn't taken his bicycle and he ran, yes, ran like a boy through the streets, devastated at the thought that, for want of fuel, the ship was going to miss the tide and perhaps fail to make its voyage to Riga. Popinga didn't sail himself, but he had passed his sea captain's examinations and what had happened filled him with shame for the firm, for himself, and for the entire shipping business.

Perhaps Mr. Julius de Coster was in his office. That sometimes happened. No, he wasn't—and Popinga, breathless, headed automatically toward his boss's house, a quiet, dignified house that was older and less practical than his own, like all the houses in the town proper. Only at the front door, when he was ringing the bell, did he think to throw away the stub of his cigar, as he prepared his speech . . .

Footsteps approached from very far off; a peephole in the door slid open; the impassive eye of a servant took note of him. Then Kees boldly demanded to speak to Mrs. de Coster, a real lady, the daughter of a provincial governor, and certainly not the type to interfere with business.

At last the door opened. Popinga waited for a long time at the foot of three marble steps, beside a potted palm, before he was given a sign to come up. There was an orange glow to the room, and he found himself facing a woman wearing a silk dressing gown and smoking a cigarette in a jade holder.

"What do you want? My husband left earlier to finish some urgent work at the office. Why didn't you go look for him there?"

He would never forget that dressing gown, or the brown hair coiled on the nape of her neck, or the woman's supreme indifference as he beat a stammering retreat.

———

Half an hour later, any hope that *Ocean III* would be leaving was gone. Kees had returned to the office, thinking that perhaps he'd missed his boss on the way. Heading home, he took a busier street: Christmas was approaching, and the shops were still open. Someone shook his hand.

"Popinga!"

"Claes!"

Dr. Claes, a pediatrician, was a member of his chess club.

"You're not coming to the tournament tonight? It looks like the Pole's going to lose . . ."

No, he wouldn't be there. His night was Tuesday in any case;

this was Wednesday. His face was flushed from running in the cold. His lungs burned.

"By the way," added Claes, "Arthur Merkemans stopped by to see me a little while ago."

"What nerve!"

"That's what I said to him..."

And Dr. Claes went off to the club, while Popinga was burdened with one more annoyance. Why did people feel they had to talk to him about his brother-in-law? Doesn't every family have something to be ashamed of?

Not that Merkemans had done anything especially wrong. His biggest fault was having eight children, though at the time he'd had a pretty good job in a salesroom. Then one day, out of the blue, it was gone. He'd been unemployed for a long time, because he was too picky, after which he'd changed course and taken every job that came along while things just went from bad to worse.

Now the whole world knew about him, because he went around begging for money and telling everyone about his reverses and his eight children.

It was embarrassing. Popinga felt a sudden knot in his stomach, and he mentally reprimanded his brother-in-law: He'd let himself go! His wife didn't even wear a hat to the market!

Too bad! Kees entered a shop and bought another cigar. He'd go home by way of the station: it wasn't much longer than by the canal. He knew he wouldn't be able to keep himself from saying to his wife, "Your brother went to see Dr. Claes."

She'd know what he meant. She'd sigh but she wouldn't say a word. That was how it always was.

Meanwhile, he walked past St. Christopher's Church and turned left into a quiet street where the snow was heaped along the sidewalks and there were heavy doors with knockers. He meant to think about Christmas, but it was hardly worth the trouble, and after the third gaslight, he knew there were other thoughts lying in wait.

Oh, nothing serious. A momentary disturbance whenever he passed this way after a game of chess...

Groningen is a sober town. There's no risk of shameless women propositioning you in the street, the way they do in places like Amsterdam.

And yet there's one house, bourgeois, prosperous-seeming, and not a hundred yards from the station, where the door opens at a tap.

Kees had never set foot inside. He'd only heard the stories people told at the club. For his part, one way or another, he'd always avoided being unfaithful to his wife.

But when he walked by the place at night, he would imagine things, and this time, after glimpsing Mrs. de Coster in her dressing gown, he was even more excited than usual. He'd never laid eyes on her except from afar, and then she'd been dressed to go out. He knew she was a mere thirty-five, while Julius de Coster the Younger was sixty.

He passed the house, pausing for an instant when he caught sight of two shadows moving behind the blinds on the second floor... He could already make out the station, from which the last train would be leaving at five after twelve... In front of the station, on the right, was the Little Saint-George, which for Kees represented something almost as reprehensible, if not quite so exciting, as the house he'd just left behind him.

Back in the days of the stagecoach, there'd been an inn called the Great Saint-George. Not far away, a bar had opened under the sign of the Little Saint-George.

Now only the little bar remained—in the cellar, its windows at sidewalk level. It was almost always empty. Only English and German sailors went there—after all the other dives had closed for the night.

There wasn't much to see, but Popinga never could resist a glance inside at the black oak tables, the benches, and the stools, and, in back, the bar with the enormous bartender behind. He had a goiter that made it impossible for him to wear a shirt collar.

Why did the Little Saint-George seem like such a den of iniquity? Because it stayed open until two or three in the morning? Because there were more bottles of gin and whiskey on its shelves than anywhere else? Because the bar was in a cellar?

On this occasion, as on all the others, Kees peeked in; a moment later his nose was glued to the window-glass. He had to get a better look—to make sure there was no mistake, or else to assure himself that there was.

Groningen possessed two kinds of establishment: the *verlof,* which served nonalcoholic drinks, and the *vergüning,* where liquor was available.

Kees considered it a disgrace just to set foot in a *vergüning.* Hadn't he given up playing skittles because the game took place in the back room of an establishment of that sort?

And the Little St. George was the most *vergüning* of them all. But there in the basement, a man was drinking—none other than Mr. Julius de Coster the Younger himself!

If Kees had rushed straight back to the chess club to tell Dr. Claes, or anyone, that he'd just seen Julius de Coster at the Little St. George—well, they would have looked at him in pity. They would have told him to take better care of himself.

There are people it's safe to joke about, but Julius de Coster...

With his chilly little goatee, the chilliest thing in all Groningen! And his aloof bearing! His black clothes! His celebrated hat, halfway between a bowler and a top hat...

No! It was impossible! Julius de Coster had shaved off his goatee? Unbelievable! Just like the badly fitting chestnut-colored suit in which he'd decked himself out!

As for finding him there, at a table in the Little St. George, in front of a heavy glass that could only be filled with gin...

Just then the man happened to turn toward the window; he was also surprised. Thrusting his head forward he recognized Popinga, his nose still pressed to the pane.

And odder still: the man motioned to him abruptly, as if to say, "So come on in."

And Kees went in: he was hypnotized, as animals are said to be by a snake. He went in and the bartender, who was wiping glasses, yelled at him from behind the bar, "You can't shut the door behind you like everybody else?!"

———

It was him—Julius de Coster! He waved his companion over to a stool and said in a low voice, "You went on board, didn't you?"

Without waiting for an answer, he used an expression that had never been heard from him before: "I bet they were really pissed off."

Finally—again no transition—"How did you know I was here? You must have been spying on me!"

What threw Kees off completely was that de Coster wasn't angry: he spoke without a sign of resentment, and an amused smile played on his lips. He signaled to the bartender to refill their glasses, then decided to keep the bottle.

"Listen, Mr. de Coster, tonight—"

"Have a drink first, *Mr.* Popinga."

He usually called Kees "mister," as he did even the least of his workers. But tonight there was something ironic about it. He seemed to be enjoying his employee's confusion.

"If I advise you to take a drink—and I heartily advise you to drink the bottle dry if you can—it's because liquor can only help in digesting what I have to say. I had no idea that I would have the pleasure of meeting you here tonight. You'll notice that I've had a bit to drink myself. That should add even greater charm to our conversation..."

He was drunk—Popinga could have sworn it. But he was drunk like a man who was used to it. Like a man who knew how to handle his liquor.

"So inconvenient, this business about the *Ocean III*! A fine ship and due to be in Riga in a week. But what's happened is in fact a great deal more inconvenient for others—for you, for example, *Mr.* Popinga."

He poured himself another drink as he spoke and drank it down. Kees noticed a large, soft package on the bench at his side.

"It's all the more inconvenient that you probably have no savings and are sure to find yourself on the street, like your brother-in-law."

So he was also bringing up Merkemans?

"Come on, drink up. You're a reasonable man, reasonable enough, so I can tell you the whole story. Imagine, *Mr.* Popinga —tomorrow morning the company of Julius de Coster and Son will be bankrupt, bankrupt due to fraudulent activity. The police will be after me."

It was lucky that Popinga had drunk two glasses of gin, one right after the other. He could make believe that the alcohol was blurring his vision, that this man with a slight smile of diabolical cynicism, who was rubbing his freshly shaved chin with such satisfaction, couldn't possibly be Julius de Coster.

"You're not going to understand a word of what I'm about to tell you because you're a true Dutchman. Later on, though, you'll think about it, *Mr.* Popinga."

He repeated "*Mr.* Popinga" in a different tone each time, as if to savor the syllables.

"First of all, let this be a lesson to you that, despite your fine qualities and the excellent opinion you have of yourself, you're a miserable manager. After all, you never noticed a thing. For more than eight years now, *Mr.* Popinga, I've been engaged in speculations that anyone would have called, to put it mildly, risky."

It was even hotter here than at Kees's house, and the heat was brutal, aggressive, the unalloyed heat of the cast-iron stoves found in tiny train stations. The air stank of gin. There was saw-dust on the floor and little rings of moisture on the table.

"Come on, drink up! You know, you'll always have drink to console yourself with! Yes, the last time I saw your brother-in-law, I had the impression that he was beginning to figure it out . . . So, you went on board and—"

"I went to your house as well."

"Where you saw the charming Mrs. de Coster. Was Dr. Claes there as well?"

"But—"

"Don't bother yourself about it, Mr. Popinga. It's almost three years to the day—it started on Christmas Eve—since Dr. Claes started sleeping with my wife."

He drank and smoked his cigar with little puffs, looking more and more, to Kees, like those Gothic devils that orna-ment the porticoes of some churches—the ones you have to shield the children's eyes from.

"As for me, it must be said that I paid a visit to Pamela in Amsterdam every week. Do you remember Pamela, *Mr.* Po-pinga?"

Was he really drunk? You had to wonder, since he stayed so cool, while Kees, like an idiot, blushed at the sound of Pamela's name.

Hadn't Popinga wanted to have her, just like everybody else? In Groningen there was just the one house of prostitution—

just one nightclub where people stayed up dancing until one in the morning.

He'd never been inside, but he'd heard all about Pamela, the buxom, brown-haired bar girl with a lisp who'd spent two years in Groningen traipsing around town in extravagant outfits that made the ladies turn away.

"Well, I was the one who paid for Pamela. I set her up in Amsterdam, at the Carlton, and then she introduces me to all her charming girlfriends. Are you beginning to get it, *Mr. Popinga*? You're not yet too drunk to take in what I'm telling you? I can only hope you'll profit from the occasion! Tomorrow, when you think about all this, you'll be a changed man. Maybe you'll make something of yourself."

He laughed. He downed his drink and poured out a glass for himself and one for his companion, whose eyes were beginning to glaze over.

"I know it's a lot at once, but I won't have an opportunity to give you a second lesson. Learn what you can. You've been such a fool, haven't you? You want evidence? Here's a professional matter. You have your sea-captain's license and you're proud of it. The company of Julius de Coster owns five clippers, and you made them your particular business. And yet you never noticed that one of them was running nothing but smuggled goods and that another was scuttled at my personal direction to collect on the insurance."

That was when something unexpected happened. In spite of himself, Kees regained his composure; he felt almost preternaturally calm. Was it the liquor? In any case, he was no longer appalled. He appeared to be listening quite calmly to everything he was being told.

Yet . . . nothing but the names of the company's five clippers. *Eleonore I . . . Eleonore II . . . Eleonore III . . .* And so on up to five. Always the name of Mrs. de Coster, the woman Kees had just glimpsed in her dressing gown, a long cigarette holder in her lips, the woman who, according to her husband, was sleeping with Dr. Claes!

And still the sacrilege wasn't complete. Above Julius de Coster the Younger and his wife there was a being who seemed exempt from every mischance—Julius de Coster the Elder, the founder of the company, who in spite of his eighty-three years still came in every day to sit enthroned in his spartan office.

"I bet," his son was now saying, "you don't even know how that old crook made his fortune. It was during the Boer War. He shipped down there all the defective munitions he could buy cheaply from arms factories in Belgium and Germany. Now he's completely senile, so much so that you have to hold his hand when he signs anything. Another bottle! Drink up, dear *Mr.* Popinga. Tomorrow, if you so please, you can communicate the entire substance of this conversation to our fellow citizens. As to me—I'll be officially dead!"

Kees must have been completely drunk, yet he didn't miss a single word or facial expression. It was like a scene from some utterly unlikely other world that he'd wandered into by mistake. Once outside, he'd be back on the solid ground of life.

"In the end, it's for your sake that I'm really upset. Remember you were the one who insisted on investing all your savings in the firm. You'd have been insulted if I'd refused. And you were the one too who wanted to build a nice big house on a twenty-year mortgage, so that now, if you don't meet the payments..."

And then he gave a shocking demonstration of his presence of mind. "In fact," he asked, "isn't the next payment due at the end of the month?"

His employer really seemed to be cut to the quick.

"I swear I did all I could. It was just bad luck, that's all. I made a bet on sugar and everything came crashing down, and I guess I'd rather start from scratch somewhere else than fight it out with all these pompous asses. I'm sorry—I'm talking for my sake more than yours. You're a decent sort, and if you'd been raised differently...Cheers, my dear Popinga!"

This time, he hadn't said "*Mr.* Popinga."

"Believe me. People aren't worth all the trouble we go through to make them think well of us. They're stupid. It's the ones who force you to look like you're virtuous who treat you the worst. I don't mean to upset you, but that makes me think of your daughter—I happened to notice her last week. Well, between you and me, she doesn't look very much like you, with her dark hair and sleepy eyes...I really have to wonder if she's actually yours...But so what? Who cares? It doesn't mean a thing if you can fool yourself! Though if you go on playing by the rules and keep getting taken..."

He was no longer speaking to Kees, but to himself. He concluded, "It just makes a lot more sense if you're the one who does the cheating! What's there to lose? Tonight I'm going to dump the clothes of Julius de Coster the Younger by the side of the canal. Tomorrow everyone will think I killed myself rather than go on living in disgrace, and those idiots will spend God knows how much money dragging the canal. Meanwhile, the 12:05 train will have taken me far, far away. Hey!"

Kees started, as if he was waking up from a dream.

"Try, if you're not too drunk, to grasp what I'm telling you. Above all, I want you to know that I'm not attempting to buy you off. De Coster would never buy anyone off, and if I've taken you into my confidence and told you all these things, that's because I know you would never even think of telling anyone else. Agreed? Now I'm going to put myself in your shoes. The fact is, you no longer have a penny to your name, and, since I know the people at the bank, I know that the minute you miss a payment they'll repossess your house. Your wife will hate you. Everyone will think you were in it with me. Whether or not you find a new job, you'll be reduced to the same state as your brother-in-law, Merkemans. I have a thousand florins in my pocket. If you stay in Groningen, there's nothing I can do for you. You won't get out of this business with half that. But if, by any chance, between now and tomorrow you start to understand ... Well, here you go!"

And, unexpectedly, de Coster pushed half the wad of money toward his companion.

"Take it! It's not everything I have. I'm not through yet, and it won't be long before I'm back on my feet. Wait! Every day for the last thirty-five years I've read the *Morning Post*, and I'm sure I'll go on reading it. If you don't stay here and if one day you need helping, place an ad in the personals signed 'Kees.' That'll be enough. Now shake hands. I hate leaving like this, on my own, like a beggar. Bartender, what do I owe?"

He paid, picked up his package by the string, and helped his companion to his feet.

"We'll avoid the brightly lit streets. Imagine, Popinga! Tomorrow I'll be dead—the best thing that can ever happen to a man!"

They walked by the famous "house," but it meant nothing to Kees, who was sunk in thought and barely keeping his balance. He'd offered to carry the package for his boss—it was a final reflexive gesture—but been rebuffed.

"Over this way—it's quieter."

The streets were deserted. Apart from the Little St. George, the "house," and the train station, Groningen was fast asleep.

From then on everything was a dream. They found themselves on the bank of the Wilhelmina Canal, not far from one of the *Eleonore*s, *Eleonore IV*, laden with cheese bound for Belgium. The snow was hard as ice. Automatically Kees caught hold of his boss, who nearly slipped as he set his old clothes down on the bank. Briefly Kees caught sight of the celebrated hat, but he didn't feel like smiling.

"Now, if you're not too worn out, you could escort me to the train. I bought a third-class ticket."

It was a true night train, somnolent and seedy. There was no one at the far end of the platform, and the stationmaster, wearing his orange helmet, was impatient to blow his whistle and head off to bed.

In one compartment a bunch of Italians lay sprawled among shapeless bundles. What brought them there? A young man in a thick overcoat, escorted by two porters, made a dignified entry into a first-class compartment; he took off his gloves and searched his pockets for loose change.

"You won't come with me?"

De Coster was laughing as he said it, and yet Kees felt a knot in his chest. In spite of his drunkenness—maybe because of it—there was a lot he knew, a lot he wanted to say...

No! This wasn't the time. And then, it wasn't quite right—Julius de Coster would think he was just showing off.

"No hard feelings, old friend—I tell you, that's life. Think about that personal ad in the *Morning Post*. But not too soon, because I'll need time to—"

Just then the train began to stir: the cars jerked forward, then back. Kees Popinga never remembered how he made it back home, or how he managed to see, one last time, the shadows behind the blinds of the "house," on the third floor now, or, finally, how he got undressed without Mother noticing anything the least bit unusual.

Five minutes later, the bed began to rock to a horrifying rhythm. All Kees could do was hang on to the covers, with the terrified feeling that at any moment he'd be dumped into the Wilhelmina Canal. And the men on the *Ocean III* wouldn't lift a finger to fish him out.

2

How Kees Popinga, in spite of sleeping badly, wakes up in a good mood; how he hesitates between Eleonore and Pamela.

USUALLY Kees slept badly when he slept on his left side. He would be gripped by a sensation of oppression, his breathing would become labored, and he would toss and turn and groan until at last he woke Mrs. Popinga up. It was she who firmly steered him back into a more comfortable position.

But he'd just slept on his left side, and he couldn't remember having had a single bad dream. Better yet: though it was often hard for him to get out of bed in the morning, now, in the blink of an eye, he was wide awake.

What woke him up was Mrs. Popinga climbing out of bed with a squeak. Kees didn't bother to open his eyes. On other days he would have immediately fallen back asleep, knowing that a full half-hour's rest still lay ahead.

But not this time. His wife went to the mirror to take out her hairpins. Cautiously, he decided to watch.

She didn't know she was being watched. Her movements were unobtrusive: she didn't want to wake her husband. She went into the bathroom, where she switched on the light. Now and then, Kees caught a glimpse of her in the frame of the doorway.

The man hadn't yet come to extinguish the gaslights, but you could hear the shovels scraping the snow away. The maid could never move without making a racket; downstairs she seemed to be battling with her stove and pots and pans.

Mother, dreamy-eyed, was putting on her long johns with the elastic bands that hermetically sealed them above the knees. She walked around, brushing her teeth, spitting and making a funny face, performing all the little rituals of daily life without knowing that she was being watched.

An alarm clock went off in the boy's room; other noises followed. Kees lay snug on his back. He thought about it, and he decided not to get up.

There! It was the first significant decision of the day. Since the company of Julius de Coster had collapsed, why should he bother to get up? It amused him to think how distraught his wife would be when he informed her that he'd be staying in bed.

Too bad! Poor old Mother would be seeing a lot more of that kind of thing!

And when it came to Mother, Kees recalled something that struck him as very much to the point. One day, five years ago, he'd bought a mahogany rowboat that he'd baptized the *Zeedeufel*, the "demon of the sea." Without prejudice he could say that it truly was a little marvel, polished, gleaming, with copper fittings and beautiful lines, a jewel of a boat.

It had been very expensive, and Kees had been almost drunk with delight. That evening, he'd complacently taken stock of their possessions: the house, the furniture, the cupboards filled with linen, the silver place settings...

That evening everyone in the household had been feeling so full of themselves that they started to joke about what would happen if, suddenly, they were ruined.

"Sometimes I think about it," Mother had imperturbably declared. "First of all, we'd have to sell everything and put the children up in a nice but not too expensive boardinghouse. Kees, I'm sure you could find a place on another ship, and I'd go to Java where I could oversee the housekeeping at a grand hotel. Do you remember Maria's aunt, who lost her husband? That's what she did, and now it seems that she's doing pretty well."

When you thought about it, you almost had to laugh: "So that's it. We're ruined! Time to count sheets and napkins in a big Javanese hotel!"

There you had it—try to see the future, and you just end up saying stupid things. Now their house and everything they owned was going to be taken from them—right in the middle of a full-blown international economic crisis, it was hardly the time to be looking for work on a ship.

Anyway, that was the last thing Popinga had in mind. And if he'd had to say what he did want, well, then he would have been forced to respond: Eleonore de Coster—or Pamela.

Right now, that was what surfaced from among the events of the night before: Eleonore with her silk dressing gown, with her long cigarette holder, her dark hair against her neck... Then the idea of Dr. Claes, a friend, someone he played chess with...

And Pamela, down in Amsterdam, who collected young girls for the sole pleasure of Julius de Coster, a satrap.

The windows were white and starred with frost. The boy had gone downstairs. School started at eight, so he must be having his breakfast. Frida was tidying her room—slowly and methodically, like her mother.

"It's seven-thirty, Kees!"

Mother was there, in the door frame. Popinga made her call to him twice before stretching and announcing, "I'm not getting up this morning."

"Are you feeling sick?"

"I'm not sick—I'm just not getting up."

He was in a mood to joke around. Aware of the enormity of his decision, he watched from between his eyelids as his wife approached the bed. Her features were frozen in disbelief.

"What's the matter, Kees? Aren't you going to the office today?"

"No."

"Have you told Mr. de Coster?"

"No."

The important thing was that he felt completely at ease. This was the real him. Yes—this is how he should have acted all along.

"Listen, Kees . . . you woke up in a bad mood. If you're feeling sick, be honest with me, but don't frighten me for nothing."

"I'm not feeling sick and I'm not getting up. Send up some tea, all right?"

De Coster himself couldn't have made sense of it. He thought that Kees would be devastated by his revelations. He wasn't the least bit devastated.

He was simply amazed, that's all, amazed that someone, most of all his boss, had the very same ideas, or dreams, that he had—because for Kees they had remained just that—dreams.

Trains, for instance. He wasn't a child anymore and it wasn't the machinery that fascinated him. If he preferred night trains, it was because they struck him as somehow strange, a little sordid. It seemed the people who left by night left forever—especially when he watched poor families piling into third class with all their baggage . . . like the Italians last night.

In other words, Kees had always dreamed of being something other than Kees Popinga. That explained why he was so completely the way he was—so completely Kees Popinga—and why he even overdid it. Because he knew that if he gave even an inch, nothing would stop him again.

Last evening . . . Yes, last evening, when Frida was starting her homework and Mother was working on her album . . . when he'd fiddled with the dial on the radio, smoking a cigar, and it had been too hot . . . He could have sat up and said straight out, "My God, I'm bored to death!"

It was to keep from saying it, or even thinking it, that he'd looked at the stove and told himself it was the handsomest stove in all Holland, that he'd looked at Mother, persuading himself that she looked good, that he'd decided his daughter had the eyes of a dreamer . . .

And again, walking by that house of ill-repute . . . Probably, if he'd gone in there even once, it would have been all over with him. He would have gone back. He would have kept women like Pamela. He might even have done something that was forbidden, because he had a lot more imagination than de Coster the Younger.

The front door opened and then closed again; a bicycle bell could be heard, Carl's bicycle bell, as he headed off to school. In fifteen minutes, Frida would be leaving, too.

"Here's your tea . . . it's very hot. Are you sure you're all right, Kees?"

"Absolutely sure."

Which was quite a stretch, he now realized. As long as he'd been lying without moving under the covers, he'd been just fine, but when he tried to sit up to drink his tea, he'd suddenly felt a stabbing pain in his neck. He came close to fainting.

"You're white as a sheet. You didn't have any problems with *Ocean III*, did you?"

"Me? Not at all."

"Aren't you going to tell me what's wrong?"

"Okay, I'll tell you. What's wrong is, *I want you to leave me the fuck alone!*"

It was beyond belief—like meeting Julius de Coster at the Little St. George. Words of that sort had never been uttered in that house, which must have been shaken to its foundations. And the thing was, he spoke them without anger. He was completely collected, as if asking for a little more tea or some sugar.

"You'll be so good, Mother, as to spare me further questions. I am forty years old. Perhaps I can begin to look after myself."

She hesitated before leaving and couldn't keep herself from plumping his pillow. With an anguished look, she noiselessly shut the door.

"I bet she's going to cry," he thought, hearing her stop on the landing.

He wasn't sick and it wasn't Sunday, but there he was in bed, at this hour, which was unsettling in its own right. Frida left in turn, and hours passed that he'd never spent in the house; he heard the milk delivered and the cleaning beginning below—things that before he'd only known about in theory.

Definitely Eleonore was the one he really wanted. Then again, he didn't think he had much of a chance. Not that he wasn't as good as Dr. Claes. They were the same age and he beat him all the time at chess. Plus Claes smoked a pipe, and most women don't like that.

Pamela—that would be a lot easier, especially now that he knew.

To think that she'd lived in Groningen for two years and he'd never had the nerve!

He got up, struck by an idea. He felt dizzier than ever and there was the same stabbing pain in his neck, but he made his way barefoot across the linoleum floor.

He wanted to make sure his wife hadn't taken his suit to be brushed. Because if she had, she'd check the pockets and find the five hundred florins.

His jacket lay on a chair. Kees took the money out and slipped it under his pillow. Back in his warm bed, he almost fell asleep.

Yes, Pamela would be better...Why had de Coster mentioned to him that his daughter Frida had dark hair and didn't look like him?

It was true. Never mind that it was difficult to imagine a woman like Mother cheating on him from the very start of their marriage.

Ever since the Spanish occupation there'd been legions of dark-haired people in Holland. And traits like that skipped generations, right?

But it was all the same to him. That's what would have surprised Julius de Coster, who thought he'd dealt him such a blow. *It was all the same to him!* The moment there'd been a little change of plan—the moment he'd lost his job and his house—from that moment on everything else could come crashing down too.

He'd smoke a pipe like Claes, eat lousy cheese, and hang out in every low dive in town. He'd order gin without a trace of embarrassment.

Suddenly there was a ray of sunlight shining through the polka-dot muslin curtain, it slanted across the room and shimmered in the mirror on the armoire door. Downstairs, the two women were fussing with their buckets and rags. Mother must be listening for him from time to time, wondering what he was up to.

The doorbell rang. There was a hushed conversation in the hallway. Mrs. Popinga climbed the stairs and came into the room wearing a look of apology. She sounded distressed. "They've come for the key..."

The key to de Coster's office, of course! A crowd must have gathered. They probably had all sorts of wild theories.

"My jacket...the right pocket."

"Do you want me to tell them anything?"

"Nothing at all."

"You don't have a message for Mr. de Coster?"

"No."

When you came down to it, it was amazing. No, he would never have dreamed it, not in a million years! Consider the idiotic ideas they had that one evening when in order to feel rich they'd imagined themselves ruined: the linen service in Java, getting posted as second mate to some ship.

Never! Not that, or anything else! Because it was over, all over, and it was time to take advantage of that!

In fact, he was sorry he hadn't had enough presence of mind to say so to de Coster. He'd let him do all the talking. De Coster had taken him for a fool, or at least a timid fellow incapable of making a decision, even though his decision had been as good as made.

He should have told him straight out, "Do you know what? I'm going to start over. I'm going to go find Pamela in Amsterdam."

It was an old score that he would have to settle. Maybe it didn't seem all that important. But it was urgent to Kees, because what he was most ashamed of was not even having dared. He'd walked past that house week after week, blushing like a schoolboy at his dirty thoughts, when instead he could have . . .

So that was all taken care of. First, Pamela. Then . . .

He'd have to see. But if Kees didn't know what he was going to do yet, he knew exactly what he wasn't going to do. That had also come up last night, though he hadn't been up to pursuing it.

Hadn't de Coster alluded to Arthur Merkemans? Hadn't he meant to offer him a word to the wise, as if to say: "Your brother-in-law, the one who hit me up for some money—what a sorry character he is!"

Kees wasn't going to turn into another Merkemans. He knew better than anyone how things stood in Groningen. Not a week went by without someone a lot more qualified than he was showing up in search of some kind—any kind—of work. The worst were the ones whose clothes weren't threadbare yet. "I was the head of this or that business," they'd say with a sigh. "Still, I'd take anything, because of my wife and children…"

Briefcase in hand, they went from company to company. Some tried to sell vacuum cleaners or life insurance.

"No!" Kees said out loud, looking at himself across the room in the mirror.

He wasn't going to wait until his suits were frayed and his shoes were falling apart, until his friends at the chess club no longer bothered to ask for his dues, since after all he was a member, with a vote on the committee, no hurt feelings and so on…

No, it wasn't going to be anything like that. True, it wasn't his fault that things had turned out this way, but since that was the way it was, he might as well take advantage of it.

"What is it now?" he yelled.

"Mrs. de Coster sent someone to ask if you know anything about her husband. It seems he never came home last night and that—"

"What am I supposed to do about it?"

"Should I tell her you don't know?"

"Tell her to go to hell! And her lover too!"

That must have set Mrs. Popinga's head spinning…

"Above all, please close the door. And tell the maid not to make so much noise with her bucket."

His head ached. He called to his wife again and asked for an orange. His mouth was dry. His tongue was thick.

The ray of sunlight shone more brightly. Outside the cold must be dry and invigorating. You could hear sounds coming from the port, the boats blowing their whistles at the first bridge of the Wilhelmina Canal. Was the *Ocean III* still at the dock? Probably. The captain must have bought fuel from a competitor, Wrichten, no doubt, who'd wonder what was up.

At the office, the staff wouldn't know what was going on. They'd be waiting for him.

He went over it all again, savoring it all in advance. First Pamela. Julius de Coster had told him she had a room at the Carlton Hotel.

After which, with his five hundred florins, he'd take a train. A night train. Maybe the *Étoile du Nord*...

How long before they discovered Julius de Coster's clothes? There was a bait and tackle shop near the place he'd left them. The black hat would stand out against the snow.

"Listen, Mother, if you bother me again, I'll—"

"Kees! It's horrible! It's unbelievable! Your boss has drowned himself! He—"

"What am I supposed to do about it?"

And, as he said it, he examined himself in the mirror to make sure his look was one of utter imperturbability. He was having fun. He used to look at himself in the mirror when he was a boy. He'd make all sorts of faces, shifting his features this way and that.

Deep down, perhaps, he'd always been an actor, and for fifteen years he'd been satisfied with the role of a good Dutchman, dignified and impassive, confident of his abilities, of his honor, of his virtue, of the high quality of all he possessed.

"How can you talk that way, Kees? Don't you understand what I just said? Julius de Coster has drowned himself!"

"So?"

"You almost make me think you know something..."

"Why do you want me to get all worked up about a man who committed suicide?"

"But he...He was your boss, and—"

"He can do what he wants, can't he? I already told you I want to sleep."

"That's impossible! There's someone from the firm down-stairs who insists on seeing you."

"Tell him I'm asleep."

"The police will come. They'll ask questions."

"So wake me up then."

"Kees! You're scaring me! You're not yourself—your eyes look different..."

"Send up some cigars, will you?"

This time she knew something must be seriously wrong with her husband. He must have been suffering from over-work. Maybe he was going a bit nuts. Patiently, she ordered the maid to bring a box of cigars: the best thing was not to contra-dict him. In the front hall, she held a long, whispered confer-ence with Kees's colleague, who left with his head bowed.

"Mr. Popinga isn't feeling well?" the maid obligingly asked as she entered the room.

"Mr. Popinga never felt better. Who told you that?"

"The missus."

It must be ten o'clock. By now all sorts of boats would be in port unloading. It would have been something to see, especially in this light, and he was sorry he was missing it, with the canal reflecting the green, red, or blue railings of the boats. Some of them would be taking advantage of the good weather by drying their sails...

Other mornings, he would have seen it all from his office. He knew all the captains and sailors. He also knew the sound of each boat's whistle. He'd say, "That's the *Jésus-Maria* passing under the second bridge—she'll be here in half an hour."

Precisely at eleven, the office boy would bring him a cup of tea and two pastries.

Meanwhile Julius de Coster the Elder would be all alone in his office with its padded doors. To think that no one knew he was senile! Plopped down in his armchair like a mummy. Like the company mascot! Clients weren't allowed to visit for more than a few seconds at a time. They took his utter vacancy for a sign of wisdom.

Kees tossed and turned in the sheets. They were getting damp. He'd soaked the armpits of his pajamas through. Still he hesitated to rise. When he did, it would be time to act.

Here, lying in his room, he could let it all play out in his head. Pamela seemed near at hand; Eleonore de Coster, in spite of her flashy cigarette holder, didn't intimidate him in the least.

But what would happen when he put on the gray uniform of Kees Popinga? When he found himself back on his feet, freshly shaved and washed, hair cream plastering his blond hair to his head?

Already he was struggling with his curiosity and with another feeling, hard to define. He wasn't going to go and get himself mixed up in the whole situation. The captain of the *Ocean III* was a crude, brutal fellow. Kees knew that. He was entirely capable of stirring up the whole port and claiming financial damages.

What if the police really turned up at the office?... The prospect was so unthinkable there was no saying how things might turn out... The whole ground floor was taken up with the warehouse; the goods were stacked to the ceiling. The employees wore blue canvas aprons.

In one corner of the warehouse, behind glass, was an office with a window that looked out onto the harbor: Kees's office. He was the conductor of the orchestra.

On the second floor there was additional storage space, plus some offices. There were yet more offices on the third above a six-foot sign on which the words JULIUS DE COSTER AND SONS —SHIPCHANDLERS figured in black on white.

Kees steeled himself to stay in bed. At the same time, he was annoyed at having been left alone for so long, even if he had ordered them not to disturb him.

The patch of sunlight had gradually spread to cover the entire surface of the mirror, and Kees began to feel more and more like the old Kees Popinga. He started to worry about all sorts of things. He wished he could chase them from his thoughts.

What were the two women doing down there? Why weren't they making noise anymore? And why hadn't they come upstairs to ask him more about his boss's suicide?

Obviously, he wasn't going to say a word, but he was still put out that they hadn't come to ask.

He ate his orange without using a knife and threw the peels on the floor to annoy Mother; then he slipped back under the covers and let his head fall back onto his pillow. He closed his eyes. He forced himself to think about Pamela and all the things he was going to do with her.

The whistle of a train came like a promise; half asleep, he'd already made up his mind not to leave during the day. That wouldn't be solitary enough. He'd wait till dusk, if not later. Dusk, which fell around four o'clock.

Pamela was a brunette, like Eleonore, but more buxom. Mrs. Popinga was stout. She always felt something like shame when Kees approached her at night. She jumped at every little sound, afraid that the children were going to hear.

Kees tried to fix his thoughts on Pamela, but in spite of himself, he kept seeing the house of de Coster and Son, odd corners of the port, boats loading and unloading. When he realized what was happening he rolled over onto the other side, heavily, and tried again: "When I get to her apartment in the Carlton, I'll say to her..."

Moment by moment, he reviewed the whole scene in advance.

"Father?"

He'd fallen asleep—that was obvious, because now he sat up with a start. He looked at his daughter with surprise. She was sniffling.

"What did you do to Mama?"

"Me?"

"She's crying. She says that something's wrong with you, that bad things are happening!"

It was awful!

"Where is your mother?"

"In the dining room. We're about to sit down for lunch. Carl is home. Mama told me not to come up…"

Frida was crying without crying—one of her little specialties. When she was a girl, she'd had the same habit. Without any provocation, she would burst into tears, a victim of the cruel world. Somebody would insist on something or tell her no or look at her reproachfully, and she'd completely fall apart.

But it was so prompt and predictable that you had to wonder just how upset she could be.

"Is it true that Mr. de Coster is dead?"

"What does that have to do with me?"

"Mama says you're sick."

"Me?"

"She wants to call Dr. Claes, but she's afraid you'll get mad."

"She's right about that. I don't need Dr. Claes, I don't need anyone."

What a strange girl! Kees had never understood his daughter. He understood her even less now. What was she doing, looking at him in bed with those big frightened eyes? What harm had he ever done to her?

Tears or no tears, she also had quite a knack for bringing things back down to earth.

"What am I going tell Mama? Will you be coming down to eat?"

"I'm not coming down."

"Should we go ahead and eat without you?"

"Yes! Go ahead! Eat! Cry! But for God's sake, leave me alone!"

He didn't feel any remorse. That wasn't it. It was annoying. He ought to have left in the morning, as if nothing had happened, as if he was setting out for work like any other day.

By now he wasn't even sure what to do. He foresaw lots of difficulties. On top of everything, he dreaded the arrival of his brother-in-law, Merkemans, who with fake concern would promise all sorts of help. Because that was how he was. Nobody could die in the neighborhood without his showing up to comfort the family.

"Go on, eat. Leave me alone."

What he needed was a stiff drink or two!

But there was nothing to drink in the house. Just a decanter of bitters, for grand occasions, or when somebody happened to drop in. That they kept under lock and key in the left-hand cupboard of the sideboard!

"Good-bye, Frida."

"Good-bye, Papa."

He spoke with a definite meaning though he hadn't intended to. She didn't pick up on it, however. She didn't feel how his eyes followed her to the door, either. He buried his face in his pillow.

The truth was he just didn't know—not any longer. Between Pamela and everything else, he could hardly keep his thoughts straight.

Luckily, at two o'clock he learned that the police were in the de Coster offices. They wanted to speak with him.

He dressed with care and examined himself closely in the mirror. Then he went downstairs. He gave his wife a long look.

"Don't you think it would be better if I came along?" she ventured.

That was what saved him. Up till then, he hadn't been sure. But the fact that she sensed danger, though she had no reason to, and that she was getting ready for it...

"I'm old enough to look after myself."

Her eyes and nose were red, the way they always were when she'd been crying. She didn't dare look him in the face. She had to know something was up.

"Are you taking your bicycle?"

"No!"

She hardly ever spoke to him using the informal *tu,* but sometimes it happened—on important occasions.

"Why are you crying?" he asked impatiently.

"I'm not."

Not crying—though the tears were rolling down her cheeks.

"You idiot!"

She'd never understand what he'd meant by that, never understand that those two words were the tenderest he'd spoken to her in is life.

"You won't be home too late?"

He was about to cry as well—that was the really stupid thing. The five hundred florins were in his pocket. In the room there were two hundred more to pay a bill that came due the day after tomorrow. He hadn't touched them.

"Do you have your gloves?"

He'd forgotten them. She brought them to him but she didn't kiss him: in their house that just wasn't done. She stayed at the door, though, and she looked a little stooped. Kees walked away, the snow crunching under his galoshes.

It took all the will in the world not to turn back.

3

About a cheap little red leather notebook bought one day
after a victory at chess.

IT WAS fifteen minutes since the train had pulled out of Groningen. There was nothing to see outside: it was four-thirty and night had already fallen. Kees Popinga was sitting in a second-class compartment with two other people: a thin little man who must have been a bailiff or clerk of some sort and, in the opposite corner, a woman of a certain age who was dressed in mourning.

Kees reached into his pocket, and his hand happened upon a little red-leather notebook, trimmed with gold, that he'd bought to keep a record of his most challenging games of chess.

There was nothing remarkable about his finding it. He was just passing the time. In the notebook there were still only two entries—two pages covered with the conventional signs.

He removed the pencil from its place in the binding and wrote: "Left Groningen on the 4:07 train."

Then he put the notebook back in his pocket. He took it out again after they left Sneek: "Stop too short to have a drink."

Much later, psychiatrists would use that notebook and those jottings to establish that Kees was insane from the moment he left Groningen.

What about his wife, who cherished her girlish diary and who, in the evening, when she ran out of pictures to paste into her album, set down in all seriousness, "Bought new shoes for Carl. Frida went to the hairdresser"—was she insane?

But it wasn't just the notebook. His fellow passengers paid no attention to him at the time. Later, however, they all had things to remember.

And there was nothing about him that would have excited curiosity. He was calm, maybe a little too calm. He thought so himself. It reminded him of two other episodes in his life when he'd displayed the same kind of effortless and unshakable sangfroid.

It was the red notebook that brought to mind the first of these incidents, since it involved a chess game. One night, he'd won three matches in a row at the chess club. Copenghem, an old man who detested him, had sneered, "There's nothing to it—once you've decided only to take on players who aren't as good as you."

Popinga, stung to the quick, had snapped back, and a challenge rapidly ensued: Kees agreed to spot Copenghem a pawn and a rook.

He could still relive the game, one of the most celebrated in the annals of the club. Copenghem was an excellent player, but Popinga had maintained an attitude of total confidence. He even got up and walked around between moves, infuriating his opponent. A new barrel of Munich beer had come in that evening, and Kees had a glass at his side.

There was no letup in Kees's aggressive irony, but after an hour, he had suddenly found himself mated. Copenghem wore a thin smile.

It was hard to imagine anything more utterly disagreeable. Twenty people or more had been watching the match. They'd seen how he carried on.

But Popinga didn't flinch. He didn't lose color or blush. On the contrary, he had been unnaturally calm. "These things happen, don't they?" he'd said in a pleasant voice.

Meanwhile, without attracting any attention, he palmed a bishop. The set was ivory. It was famous throughout Groningen. And it belonged to Copenghem, who would play with no other.

Popinga had nabbed the black bishop. In a flash, he dropped it into his glass of Munich beer.

Another match was about to begin. The disappearance of the bishop was discovered, and it was looked for everywhere. The waiter was called, all sorts of theories were advanced, but nobody thought to look in the glass of dark beer and Kees was careful not to drink it. God knows where it had been emptied out finally. In any case, Copenghem never retrieved his bishop.

Through it all, Popinga had felt as calm as calm can be and he felt the same way now, on the train. He was thinking about the good people of Groningen and about the trick he'd played on them by disappearing.

Which didn't stop the woman in mourning from declaring, two days later, "He looked like a hunted man. Twice he burst out laughing for no reason."

He hadn't laughed; he had smiled. First, because of Copenghem; second, because of the oxtail soup.

That had been more recent—from last year, when Jef van Duren had been named professor at the medical school. Van Duren, an old friend, had thrown a big dinner party. While the vermouth was being served, Kees had stolen into the kitchen, where he liked to flirt with Maria, the delectable maid.

He tried to fondle her, but she'd said, "If you're not going behave, I'll just have to leave the room."

And she went down to the cellar, where she had a chore to do.

He'd been mortified—all the more so because Maria was pretty much the only woman with whom he permitted himself such liberties. It never failed to bring a flush to his cheeks.

He'd stayed calm, though. Terribly calm. Remembering how he'd dropped the bishop in the beer, he noticed that on the stove there was a pot of oxtail soup, a dish that the van Durens reserved for special occasions. He saw various boxes were lined up on a shelf, including two of salt. He grabbed one and poured almost the entire contents into the oxtail soup. Then, innocent as can be, he went back to the main room.

It turned out even funnier than he'd hoped. God knows why, but the box marked SALT had been full of confectioner's sugar, and for a good minute every face around the table was rigid with astonishment. It was with furrowed brows that the guests sipped at their soup, unable to know what to make of the situation.

He felt the same kind of calm today. At six the train dropped him off in Stavoren. There was no time for a drink, although he'd been thirsty for a while. He had to run to catch the ferry across the Zuiderzee; luckily they served liquor.

"Two glasses of gin," he said to the steward. It was a perfectly natural request.

He ordered two because he knew he'd drink them both. He also knew that on the crowded boat it would be impossible to get the waiter to come a second time. Last night, at the Little St. George, Julius de Coster had told them to leave the bottle on the table. The bartender hadn't seen anything unusual in that.

And yet later the waiter would say, "He looked like a madman. He ordered two glasses of gin at once."

After the forty-minute crossing to Enkhuizen he caught the train to Amsterdam, arriving a few minutes after eight. On this last leg of his trip, he shared a compartment with two livestock dealers. They discussed business while casting suspicious glances in his direction. Possibly they took him for a competitor.

But even then he did not suspect the notoriety that he was very shortly to achieve. He was dressed, as usual, in gray. Without thinking, he'd brought his leather briefcase along—the one he always took to the office.

When it came to dropping the bishop in the beer or the sugar in the oxtail soup, he hadn't wasted a moment. In Amsterdam, he headed straight to the Carlton.

"Is Miss Pamela in?"

There was absolutely nothing to set him apart from any other visitor. His composure, perhaps.

"Whom should I announce?" asked the uniformed man at the front desk.

"Julius de Coster."

The man paused and looked at him. "Excuse me," he said in a low voice, "but you're not Mr. de Coster."

"How would you know?"

"Mr. de Coster comes every week. I know him."

"And who says I'm not another Mr. de Coster?"

The man went ahead and called up. "Hello? Miss Pamela? There's a gentleman here who's come on behalf of Mr. de Coster. Should I send him up?"

The elevator boy suspected nothing.

Pamela was combing her hair in front of the mirror. "Come in!" she said loudly, not showing much interest. Then she turned around. There'd been no response, though she'd heard the door open and close.

She saw Kees Popinga standing there, with his briefcase under his arm and his hat in hand. "Sit down, please," she said quietly.

"Thank you, no," he replied.

They were in one of the hundred or so rooms in the Carlton, all of them alike. The door into the brightly lit bathroom stood halfway open. A nightgown lay on the bed.

"De Coster asked you to tell me something? Do you mind if I keep brushing my hair? I'm late. In fact, what time is it?"

"Eight-thirty. You have lots of time."

And he put down his briefcase and hat, took off his coat, and ventured a smile at the mirror.

"You won't remember me, but I used to see you often in Groningen...and for two years I've wanted you. So yesterday de Coster and I had a little chat, and now I've come..."

"What are you talking about?"

"Don't you understand? I've come because things are different from how they were when you lived in Groningen."

He had moved closer and was standing beside her. She was annoyed, but she went on putting up her brown hair.

"It would take too long to explain. The important thing is, I've decided to take up a little of your time..."

———

Possibly he was even calmer when he left. There were six flights of stairs and he didn't take the elevator. He was all the way at the bottom before he realized that he'd left his briefcase in Pamela's room. He wondered if the man at the front desk would notice it.

Which meant Kees was thinking straight, because the man already was staring at his empty hands.

"I left my briefcase upstairs," he said matter-of-factly. "I'll be back tomorrow."

"Do you want me to send the elevator boy up?"

"Thanks, no—it's not worth the trouble."

And he took a coin from his pocket and handed it to the

man. It seemed like a clumsy gesture, though. He wasn't used to grand hotels.

Ten minutes later, he was at the station. There wasn't an express train to Paris until 11:26—two hours to go. He spent the time walking around the platforms admiring the trains.

At precisely a quarter to eleven, a little showgirl who went out with Pamela every night showed up at the Carlton. "She hasn't come down yet?" she asked. "I've been waiting a whole hour for her at the restaurant."

"I'll call her room."

The man at the desk called three times and then gave up with a sigh. "I'm sure I didn't see her go out."

He called over the elevator boy, who was walking by.

"Run up and see if Miss Pamela has drowsed off."

Popinga, on the station platform, gave no sign of impatience. He roamed around, waiting for his train. He kept himself entertained by looking over the other travelers as they went by.

The elevator boy came tearing down all six flights of stairs. He slumped onto a sofa. "Quick!" he shouted. "Up there!"

Since he'd left the elevator on the sixth floor, there was nothing to do but take the stairs. Pamela lay across her bed, a towel stuffed in her mouth. The director of the hotel had to be notified and the doctor called. It was eleven-thirty before the police also arrived. The train for Paris had just pulled out.

———

This was the real thing—a night train like the ones in Popinga's dreams, with sleeper cars and blinds on the compartment windows, with the lights dimmed and travelers speaking in many languages, a train that was truly international. They would be crossing two borders in the space of a few hours.

He'd bought a second-class ticket and found a compartment with only one passenger who was already stretched out on his seat. Kees hadn't had a chance to see his face.

He didn't want to sleep, and he didn't want to sit, so he walked the length of the train several times over. He walked slowly, trying to peer into the compartments, to guess...

The conductor punched his ticket without a glance. The Belgian police hardly bothered to look at his identity card. While they were stopped at the border, he took out his notebook and wrote: "Took the 11:26 train from Amsterdam—second class."

A little later, he felt like writing again: "I just can't understand why Pamela laughed at me when I told her I wanted to have her. It's too bad! There was no way for me to leave. Now she understands!"

If only she'd smiled at him, or made a cutting remark! If only she'd lost her temper! But no. She'd looked him over and burst into laughter, unending laughter, loud, hysterical laughter that shook her all over and made her more attractive than ever.

"You are not allowed to laugh," he'd said in a stern voice.

At which she laughed even louder, until tears came to her eyes. He grabbed her by the wrists.

"I want you to stop laughing."

He shoved her toward the bed, and she fell onto it.

The towel was there, by the nightgown, where he could reach it.

"Tickets, please!"

This time it was the Belgian conductor. He shot a glance in Kees's direction, casting a curious eye at this passenger who, in spite of the cold, remained in the corridor. But, even so, to suppose...

At the border, Kees's fellow passenger struggled awake. Kees saw that he had a small brown mustache.

What a strange night it was, for all that. It felt almost as overwhelming as the previous night, when he'd listened to de Coster at the Little St. George for hours. What would he say when he heard the news?

Would Pamela go to the authorities? In that case, Popinga's name would be all over the papers. He'd left his briefcase in her room.

The whole thing seemed incredible. There was no way to even begin to consider the consequences. Frida, for example, was in a convent school. Would they keep the daughter of a man who...?

And at the chess club! The expression on Copenghem's face! And on Dr. Claes's! Probably he thought he was the only man there with a mistress. And...

He let his eyelids drift down, his features rigidly set. Sometimes he saw lights going by outside the window, or he heard the rushing noise as they passed through a station. He made out a vast, snowy plain and a little house with all its lights on for some reason in the middle of the night. Maybe a death or a birth...

Perhaps it was just as well that he'd forgotten his briefcase at Pamela's? You had to wonder. Every moment there was something new to write in his red notebook.

He left the train at the French border to see if there was a food stand open. He had to go the long way around because of customs. He drank a big glass of brandy, then jotted down in his notebook: "I notice that alcohol no longer has an effect on me."

The last leg of the journey stretched out. Kees made an effort to strike up a conversation with his fellow passenger, who was a broker in precious stones. But the man made the same trip two or three times a week, and he preferred to sleep.

"Do you know if the Moulin Rouge will still be open?" Popinga asked him nevertheless.

He wanted to see people, so he wandered the corridors again, passing from car to car, pressing his face to the compartments full of sleeping people.

The Moulin Rouge or maybe somewhere else ... He'd brought up the Moulin Rouge because he'd read so much about it.

Already he saw himself in a room filled with mirrors. There were purple velvet banquettes and a champagne bucket on the table and pretty girls in low-cut dresses on every side. He wouldn't lose control! The champagne wouldn't affect him any more than gin or brandy. He'd feel free to make some suggestive remarks that the girls couldn't understand ...

Suddenly, without warning, they were at Gare du Nord. The concourse smelled musty. There was a taxi waiting outside.

"To the Moulin Rouge!" he spluttered.

"You don't have any luggage?"

The Moulin Rouge was closed, but the taxi stopped in front of another nightclub, where a doorman was quick to accost Popinga. No one would ever have guessed it was his first time in such a place. He didn't rush things. He looked around calmly and picked a table without paying any attention to the maître d'.

"I want champagne and a cigar!"

There you had it! Things had turned out exactly as he'd planned. It seemed altogether to be expected that a girl in a green dress would arrive to slip into a seat beside him with a murmured, "May I?"

"Please do," he replied.

"You're not from here?"

"I'm Dutch. But I speak four languages, my own, French, English, and German."

He felt a magnificent sense of fulfillment. He'd foreseen it all, down to the smallest detail. That was what was so extraordinary.

To think that he already knew all about this nightclub with its crimson velvet seats, jazz band, and a blond saxophonist who had to be a northerner and might even be Dutch, like him; that he knew all about this redhead who was leaning her elbows on the table and asking for a cigarette.

"Waiter!" he called out. "Cigarettes."

A little later he took his notebook out of his pocket. "What's your name?" he asked.

"Me? You want to write down my name? That's a funny idea! Well, if it makes you happy, Jeanne Rozier. Hey, it's almost closing time."

"Doesn't make any difference to me."

"What are you going to do?"

"Go to your place."

"My place? I'm afraid that's impossible. But what about a hotel? How about that?"

"All right by me."

"Say, you're pretty easygoing!"

He smiled a little. It was funny, though he couldn't say why.

"Do you come to Paris often?"

"This is my second time. The first was my honeymoon."

"Your wife's with you?"

"No. I left her at home."

He burst out laughing. He summoned the maître d' and ordered more champagne.

"You like your women small, don't you?"

This time, he did laugh. "Hardly!" he exclaimed.

How would she know what he meant? Pamela wasn't small —she was as big as he was. And Eleonore de Coster was something like five foot eight.

"Well, you're having a good time. Are you here on business?"

"I'm not sure."

"What do you mean?"

"Nothing. Your lipstick's smudged. It's pretty funny."

She kept darting glances at him, doing her best to figure him out, but not succeeding. That was what was funny. True, he could see patches of powder under her eyes, but her mouth was wide and her hair was red and beautiful, though a little dull. He only knew one redhead, the wife of a friend of his at the chess club. She was a tall, thin woman with a slouch and five children.

"What are you looking at me like that for?"

"No reason. It's wonderful here. I'm thinking about Pamela."

"Who?"

"It doesn't matter. You don't know her."

"Come on, pay up so we can go. Everybody's tired."

"Waiter! I need to change these florins."

And he pulled the five hundred florins out of his pocket. Unconcerned, he handed the money over.

But he was tired too. There were moments when he felt as if he absolutely had to lie down, except who was going to miss out on a day like this for the sake of a nap?

"Why can't I come to your place?"

"I've got a friend."

He gave her a suspicious look.

"What's he like? How old?"

"Thirty."

"What's he do?"

"Business."

"Ah! I'm in business, too."

He kept discovering new dimensions of himself: his face in the mirror, the way he moved, the things he had to say—he enjoyed every minute of it.

"Here you are, sir."

He'd count his change as carefully as ever, though. "Not a very good rate," he said. "I would have done better in Amsterdam."

Jeanne Rozier hesitated for a moment outside. She was wearing a squirrel-fur coat.

"Where are you staying?"

"Nowhere. I came straight from the station."

"And your luggage?"

"I don't have any."

She wondered if it wouldn't be wiser to beg off.

"What's the matter?" he asked, astonished by his own boldness.

"Nothing—come on, there's a hotel on rue Victor-Massé. It's pretty nice."

There was no snow in Paris. It didn't get cold enough there. Popinga felt as light as the champagne he'd just put away. His companion was at home in the hotel. She walked in and yelled out through a glass door, "Don't get up, I'll take room 7."

She turned down the covers and locked the door. Then she sighed.

"Aren't you going to get undressed?" she asked from the little bathroom.

After all, why not? He'd do as he was told!

He was as obedient and cheerful as a child. He wanted everyone to be happy.

"Are you staying long in Paris?"

"Maybe forever."

"And you don't have any luggage?"

She felt uneasy and undressed reluctantly. He sat on the bed, watching her with an amused look on his face.

"What are you thinking about?"

"Nothing. That's pretty. Is that a silk slip?"

Without taking it off, she slid between the sheets. She waited. The light was still on.

"What are you doing?" she asked after a moment.

"Nothing."

Finishing his cigar, that's all. He lay on his back and looked at the ceiling.

"You're not nervous?"

"No!"

"Do you mind if I turn out the light?"

"No."

She flipped the switch. She could feel him lying beside her; he hadn't moved at all. His lips closed round the butt of his cigar. It made a small red stain in the darkness.

She was the one who was nervous, not him.

She kept tossing and turning. "Why did we come here?" she finally asked.

"We're having fun."

He felt the warmth of her body at his side. It gave him a pleasure that was perfectly proper. "If only 'Mother' were here," he said to himself.

Without warning, he got up and turned on the light. He looked around for his jacket. He took out his notebook. "What's the address?" he asked.

"The address where?"

"Here. Where we are."

"Rue Victor-Massé, 37A. You need to write that down too?"

Yes! Just as some travelers collected postcards or restaurant menus. He got back into bed. He stubbed out his cigar in the ashtray and whispered, "I'm not sleepy yet. What sort of business is he in?"

"Who?"

"Your friend."

"The car business. But listen, if that's all you've got to say, I wish you'd just let me sleep. You seem like a pretty funny sort of guy. What time do you want to wake up?"

"Don't wake me up."

"All right, then. You don't snore?"

"Only when I sleep on my left side."

"So try to sleep on your right."

He was awake for a long time, with his eyes open. His companion settled into a light snore, and he laughed silently to himself.

It reminded him somehow of yesterday morning in Groningen—when he'd watched Mrs. Popinga getting dressed without her knowing.

It was daylight, but the room was still mostly dark: the sun wasn't up yet and the curtains were closed. There was only a trace of light.

Kees could see Jeanne Rozier in silhouette. She stood with his pants in one hand.

She was searching his pockets. The night before she'd noticed him stuffing his money into them. She was trying not to make a noise and there was a funny expression on her face. Popinga started to grin.

She must have sensed it somehow, in spite of his silence. She turned suddenly, and right away he closed his eyes. She wondered whether he was asleep or pretending to be.

She stood in a faint shaft of light with his pants in her hand, waiting uncertainly. She was holding her breath, afraid to move. The scene filled him with pleasure. For a moment she was taken in and she let her hand slide into another pocket. Then she knew.

"So..." Her voice trailed off.

"What?"

"Are you through making fun of me?"

"Why do you say that?"

"It's all right. I can see."

She threw the pants onto a dingy yellow chair, picked up her coat, and came over to the side of the bed.

"Are you going to tell me why you came to Paris without

any luggage but with your pockets bursting with money? Don't act like an idiot. I admit I've played along..."

"But..."

"Wait!"

And she drew the curtains from the window, letting the icy day in.

"Go on—tell me!"

She sat down on the edge of the bed and looked at him closely. Then she sighed. "I should have seen right away that there's something not right about you. Last night, when you said you're in business, what did that mean? I bet you deal coke. Tell me it isn't true!"

4

*How Kees Popinga spends Christmas Eve, and how, in the
early hours of the morning, he chooses a car that suits him fine.*

AT THE Carlton, the man at the front desk had taken him for
a madman, and now—because he hadn't lost his temper when
he caught her rifling through his pockets—Jeanne Rozier
thought he was dealing cocaine. Well, that was fine by him. For
forty years, he'd gone to a lot of trouble and never done a single
unexpected thing so that people wouldn't take him for anyone
but Kees Popinga.

"I'm tired," he muttered, without bothering to answer his
companion. She had approached the bed.

Her eyes were green and flecked with violet. He could tell
from them that she was genuinely intrigued, not just a little curious. It would bother her to leave without finding out. She
rested one knee on the bed. "Don't you want me to get back in
for a bit?" she murmured.

"Don't bother."

She was holding the bills she'd taken from his pocket. She
set them down on the table so he could see.

"Look. I'm putting them right here. But do you mind if I
take one?"

He wasn't so sleepy that he couldn't see it was a thousand-franc note. But what did it matter? He dozed off.

The morning was chilly, but it was only a short walk to the little furnished apartment on the rue Fromentin that Jeanne Rozier called home. After climbing the three flights of stairs, she went in and closed the door behind her without making a sound. She poured the cat some milk, carefully got undressed, and slid into bed. It was already occupied by a man.

"Move over a bit, Louis."

He moved over with a groan.

"I've just come from being with this weird guy. The whole thing was a little scary."

But Louis wasn't listening, and Jeanne Rozier stared at the gap in the curtains for another fifteen minutes before she fell asleep. She really was asleep this time, in her own warm bed next to Louis, who was wearing his silk pajamas.

About the same time, as people reluctantly filed into offices after smoking the day's first bitter cigarette, a telegram arrived at the rue des Saussaies:

CRIME BUREAU AMSTERDAM TO CRIME BUREAU PARIS

KEES POPINGA, AGE 39, RESIDENT GRONINGEN, SOUGHT FOR MURDER OF PAMELA MAKINSEN, COMMITTED NIGHT 23–24 DECEMBER IN ROOM AT CARLTON HOTEL AMSTERDAM. STOP. REASON TO ASSUME POPINGA TOOK TRAIN TO FRANCE. STOP. WEARING GRAY CLOTHES AND GRAY HAT. STOP. HAIR BLOND, SKIN FAIR, EYES BLUE, WEIGHT AVERAGE, DISTINGUISHING MARKS NONE. STOP. FLUENT IN ENGLISH, GERMAN, FRENCH.

Smoothly, unhurriedly, the mechanism went into motion: the bulletin concerning Kees Popinga was transmitted by radio, telegraph, and telephone to every border and to the local and national branches of the police.

In every Paris police station, a sergeant deciphered the ticker of the Morse machine: "weight average, distinguishing marks none..."

And all the while Kees Popinga, in his hotel room, lay fast asleep. He was still sleeping at noon. At one, the chambermaid knocked at the glassed-in office to ask, "Is room 7 free yet?"

No one could remember, so the maid went to check; she caught sight of Kees's face, asleep and serene, mouth open wide. Close by, on the table, lay a wad of bills that she was afraid to touch.

At four, when the streetlights had just been lit, Jeanne Rozier returned. She pushed open the office door.

"Is the guy I came with last night gone?"

"I think he's still sleeping."

Jeanne, a newspaper in her hand, climbed the stairs. She opened the door and looked at Popinga. He lay motionless as ever. His sleeping features were those of a child.

"Kees!" she called out abruptly in a tight voice.

The word reached him through his sleep, but she had to repeat it several times before he regained full consciousness. Popinga opened his eyes. He saw the light over the bed and Jeanne Rozier in a hat and squirrel-fur coat.

"You're still here." He said it indifferently.

Already he was rolling over in order to pick up the thread of his dreams. She had to shake him awake.

"Didn't you hear what I said?"

He looked at her calmly, rubbed his eyes, and lifted himself up a bit. His voice was quiet, almost as childlike as his expression while he was sleeping. "What did you say?"

"I called you Kees—Kees Popinga!"

She enunciated each of the syllables, but he didn't react.

"Don't you understand? Here—read that!"

She threw the afternoon paper on the bed and paced around the room.

A showgirl was murdered in an Amsterdam hotel.

The murderer has been identified thanks to documents left at the scene.

The perpetrator appears either to be insane or a sadistic killer.

Jeanne started to get impatient. She looked at him again and again, waiting for his reaction. He seemed unsurprised. There was no sign of strain as he said, "Do you mind handing me my jacket?"

She was naïve enough to feel the pockets to make sure it wasn't a weapon he wanted. It was a cigar! He lighted it with exasperating slowness, propped himself up on his pillow, and began to read, moving his lips from time to time.

... According to breaking news, Popinga left his house in Groningen under circumstances that raise the question of whether he may have committed another crime. His employer, M. Julius de Coster, disappeared suddenly, and ...

"So it's really you?" Jeanne Rozier hammered away at him. She'd reached the end of her patience ...

"Of course it's me."

"You strangled that woman?"

"I didn't mean to. It's hard for me to believe that she died. Anyway, the article exaggerated a lot. Some of it simply isn't true."

He stood up and headed toward the bathroom.

"What are you doing?"

"Getting dressed. I need some lunch."

"It's five o'clock!"

"Some dinner, then."

"What are you going to do afterward?"

"I don't know."

"You're not afraid of being picked up on the spot?"

"I'd have to be recognized."

"And where are you going to sleep? Aren't you forgetting that you might be asked for your papers?"

"That would obviously be a problem."

He hadn't had time to think it through yet, and he'd slept so deeply that now he was having trouble gathering his thoughts.

"I'll figure it all out later. Meanwhile, I don't even have a toothbrush. Is today the twenty-fourth?"

"Yes."

"Don't they put up Christmas trees around here?"

"We have parties on Christmas Eve. In all the restaurants people are eating and dancing. In all the cafés ... Tell me— you're not pulling my leg?"

"Why would I?"

"I don't know! You're not putting me on, pretending to be Popinga?"

There it was again! People were practically driven, no matter what, to mistake him for someone else.

"I'm going to tell you something," Jeanne continued. "I'm not promising anything yet. It's probably stupid to get involved. I was just speaking to someone about you. Don't worry, it wasn't anyone with a connection to the cops. It was someone who, if he cared to, could get you out of this. But I don't know if it's going to work. Stories like yours are a little off-putting."

He listened as he tied his black shoes.

"I won't be seeing him until fairly late. Do you know the rue de Douai? No? It's not far—you'll have to ask. There's a tobacconist's. All you have to do is sit and wait. I'll try to make it by midnight, maybe later, because a bunch of us are having Christmas dinner."

She gave him a final look and picked up the paper from the bed.

"Don't leave it lying around like that. That's how people get caught. And I'll pay for the room myself so the office won't come bothering you. They're already amazed at how long you slept. That's one more sign."

"Sign of what?"

But she shrugged and left.

"At the tobacconist's on the rue de Douai."

Eight o'clock, the grand boulevards. Paris was beginning to stir. He stopped to look at the latest edition of an evening paper. There was a photograph on the front page with the caption PAMELA'S KILLER (by wire from Amsterdam).

Incredible! The first thing he had to wonder was where the picture had come from; he had no recollection of it. Then, looking more closely, he made out someone's cheek to the left of his head, and he knew. The other person was his wife. It was the family picture they kept on the side table.

They'd blown up his head and cropped out everything else; plus it had been transmitted by wire so the image looked smeared, as if it had been left out in the rain.

He stopped at a second newsstand: same paper; same picture. He was almost sorry it was so hard to recognize him. It could have just as well been some random passerby.

The murderer's wife claims an attack of amnesia ...

He went to a third newsstand and bought the paper. He asked, "Aren't there any other evening papers?"

Four more were pointed out. He took them all.

"What about papers from Holland?"

"At the newsstand on the place de l'Opéra."

There were bright lights all around; posters advertising Christmas dinner, the whole works, for twenty-five or a hundred francs. The big day wasn't here yet, but you could feel it approaching.

"May I see the papers from Holland, please."

He winced. Before him was the *Daily Mail.* His photograph—the same one as in the French papers—was right there on the front page.

"I'll take the *Daily Mail* and the *Morning Post.*"

The more the merrier was how he felt, just as he used to live to see the work piling up on his desk. Was it time to head over to the tobacconist's on the rue de Douai?

He thought that the best thing would be to eat dinner first and he sat down at the Café de la Paix. The waiters were hanging up the last wreaths along with bunches of mistletoe.

It reminded him that by now Amersen must have delivered the Christmas tree he'd ordered. What were they going to do at home? What would a girl like Frida make of it all?

He never used to think about such things when he read the news. Now that he himself was at the center of a news story, he'd become aware of its many ramifications.

For instance, he had a life insurance policy. What happens to life insurance when the policyholder is a murderer?

"How is everything?" the waiter asked. He'd ordered a steak, rare.

"Excellent," was his firm reply.

It was hard for him to read the papers while eating, though, and dessert wasn't the treat it was in Holland. He liked his cake sweeter. And he usually drank his coffee with whipped cream and a dash of vanilla. The waiter would have none of it.

The person he'd really made an impression on was Jeanne Rozier; he could tell, because she was looking out for him although he hadn't asked her for anything. But what was going on in her head? Obviously she though he was one cool customer. He thought so too. Just to prove it, he asked a cop on the corner of the boulevard des Capucines how to get to the rue de Douai.

There was the corner shop, with the tobacconist's counter and, set off behind a glass divider, a little café with several tables. Kees Popinga was lucky enough to find an empty one in the corner by a window, and he sat down. Outside, the nightclubs' neon signs were beginning to light up, but the bouncers and showgirls were still seated at the bar, discussing their private business. A flower vendor sat in the opposite corner. She'd set down her basket and was drinking coffee with a glass of rum.

"Waiter, a coffee for me too!"

Christmas Eve was beginning all around him, but it felt strange to him and a little disappointing, too. It didn't seem like a real Christmas Eve—more like a crazy revel. It was nine and already people were drunk in the streets! And nobody had said a word about Midnight Mass!

From our special correspondent in Groningen:
    While Amsterdam police continued their investigation at the Carlton, where the unfortunate Pamela met her death, we hastened to Groningen to learn more about the character of Kees Popinga, the showgirl's killer...

Kees sighed much as he used to do whenever an employee of the firm of Julius de Coster had made an unforgivable mistake.

He took his red notebook out of his pocket and noted down the date and the name of the newspaper. Then he wrote: "Not murderer, killer. Important to remember that the death was accidental."

He looked over at the flower vendor. She had dozed off while waiting for the people to stream out of the theaters. He went back to his paper.

We were amazed to learn that Kees Popinga was a well-known and respectable figure in town. The news has caused consternation, and everyone has his theory...

He drew a line under the word "theory." How pretentious!

The distress of the Popinga household is painful to watch. Mme Popinga was anxious to explain...

Coolly, between two puffs of his cigar, he recorded in his notebook: "In spite of everything, Mother talked to the press!"

Suddenly the flower vendor's chin dropped down onto her chest. Kees smiled.

...to explain that only an unforeseen mental collapse, a fit of amnesia, could account for the actions of...

"Actions"—that was worth underlining too, especially if Mother had really used the word.

Then he chose a blank page and wrote: "Mme Popinga's opinion: madness or amnesia."

She wasn't the only one who held that opinion. A young assistant at de Coster's, a boy of seventeen that he himself had hired, declared solemnly, "I'd already noticed the strange look he sometimes had in his eyes."

As to Claes, he had it all figured out: "Obviously Popinga's actions must be ascribed to insanity. As to whether he was predisposed to such a thing, professional confidentiality prevents me from . . ."

Plain mad! Outright insane! Some even went so far as to suggest that he'd killed Julius de Coster first.

While Old Copenghem confided: "It pains me to speak ill of a fellow member of our chess club, but to any impartial observer it must have been clear that Kees Popinga was consumed with resentment. He believed that he was better at everything than everybody else. He was scheming and he was vengeful. Everything can be explained by an inferiority complex . . ."

Popinga wrote "Inferiority complex" beside Copenghem's name. Then, in smaller letters, "Can you believe this?!—he only beat me at chess once!"

At ten o'clock he noticed that the café had filled up; he was gradually being pushed to one end of the bench. From time to time he lifted his eyes from his papers or notebook to study some stranger's face. Then, blinking, he would return to his thoughts. After a while, though, he became aware of five or six blacks in the crowd. The flower vendor was still there. Some people were dressed to go out; others were in their shabby workaday clothes.

He didn't know that he was on the fringes of Montmartre, that these were show-people. Soon the whole neighborhood would be hopping.

The employee at the Groningen train station remembers a man in a state of tremendous agitation . . .

"Not true," he wrote heatedly. They could talk all they wanted about insanity and inferiority complexes, but to claim —just because a few hours later he happened to kill Pamela—

to claim that he'd been in a state of agitation when he left Groningen ... Was he now? Even after two cups of coffee?

But worst was the man from the hotel in Amsterdam. Popinga would have gladly slapped him.

"From the moment of his arrival, I noticed something abnormal. I thought of warning Miss Pamela ..."

"So why didn't he?" Kees wrote.

"When he came down," the man went on, "it was with the air of a hunted animal, and ..."

"The air of a hunted animal!" Popinga made a note of it, adding sarcastically, "Does he have any idea what he's talking about?"

At which point he looked up, since someone was standing in front of him and looking him over. It was a young man in a dinner jacket. Jeanne Rozier stood behind him. "My friend Louis," she whispered. "I'll leave you two alone."

"Got a moment?" Louis said. His hands were in his pockets and a cigarette dangled from his lips. "Just leave that stuff there. Let's go downstairs."

He led Kees down to the bathroom in the cellar and examined him from head to toe. In a low voice he said, "Jeanne told me the whole story. I had a look at the newspapers. Tell me, do you do stuff like that often?"

Popinga smiled. From the way Louis was looking at him —straight in the eyes with a trace of irony—he could tell he wasn't talking about insanity or an inferiority complex.

"It was the first time," he said, suppressing a smile.

"And the other one, the old guy?"

"They don't know what they're talking about. Julius de

Coster had a business setback so he skipped town. He wants them all to think that he killed himself. That's the reason I—"

"That's enough. I don't have time right now. Can you drive?"

"A car? Sure."

"So, from what Jeanne tells me, you need a place to hide until you can get some new identity papers?"

He took the cigar from Popinga's lips and lit another cigarette. His tone was careless: "We'll see about that. Wait for me upstairs. A bunch of us are having dinner across the street."

It was almost midnight. The flower vendor had disappeared, along with two of the blacks. From time to time, a bouncer from one of the cabarets came in to have a drink with a taxi driver or some other character. There'd be a deal to go over, then the bouncer would head back to his post across the street.

Popinga could never have imagined such a pathetic Christmas Eve! He waited in vain for the pealing of church bells at midnight; instead a drunkard stood up in order to drone a few lines—the only ones he knew—from "O Come All Ye Faithful." The café owner decided to turn on the radio. Seconds later the room filled with the sound of organs and the voices of men and children belting out a sacred song.

Kees folded his newspaper and ordered another coffee; he still didn't feel like a drink. He stared out the window where a priest was bending over to bless a group of the faithful.

There was a girl—slim, poorly dressed—standing directly in front of him. She was white as a sheet—it must have been the cold. Every hour or so she'd come in, chilled to the bone from walking up and down the street.

Cars kept pulling up in front of the nightclubs. The black guys were arguing furiously about something.

What was so strange was that all over the world, at this hour, in all the churches . . .

Popinga imagined the world seen from a plane, a plane that

flew unbelievably high and fast: the world would look like a huge ball, white with snow, with church spires fixing the towns and villages in place like monstrous nails, and in every church, candles, incense, the hush of the faithful before the Nativity scene.

But it wasn't like that, really! For one thing, Midnight Mass was already over to the east, where by now it was one in the morning. And in America it was still day. And all over the world, outside of the churches, blacks were talking business, girls were warming up in cafés reeking of alcohol, and hotel doormen . . .

Well, he wasn't going to let himself be swept up in it all, either: he had no desire to hum along with the radio. Was the owner some kind of ex-choirboy? He'd had to turn it off, in any case. You couldn't hear yourself talk. Instead of being pleased, the customers had complained.

Suddenly the voices of the drinkers came through loud and clear: a low ceiling of blue cigarette smoke hovered beneath the white ceiling overhead. In front of Popinga a young man in a wrinkled tuxedo was sitting alone. There was a glass of mineral water in front of him, and he was stuffing white powder into his nose.

Why had Louis asked him if he knew how to drive? What if, just like that, he stood up and identified himself, in the words of one of the evening papers, as "Popinga, the Amsterdam sex fiend"? What would all these people say then?

He was still there, in the same seat, at 2 AM. The waiter was coming to know him, flashing little signs as he went by. Kees had no idea what to do with himself, so he followed the example of the young man and ordered some mineral water. The other tables were empty; he was the only person left sitting.

An argument broke out at the bar. People were shouting and someone brandished a water siphon, shattering it on a table.

People spilled out onto the sidewalk, where they milled around in confusion.

A police whistle sounded from somewhere. Popinga didn't panic; he picked up his papers and headed to the toilets, shutting himself into one of the stalls. He gave cursory attention to an article on the economic expansion of Holland during the eighteenth century.

Fifteen minutes later, he came back upstairs. Everything was quiet; the shards of the siphon had been swept up off the floor. The drinkers were all gone. The waiter came over with a wink and a nod. Kees's well-timed disappearance hadn't escaped him.

"A lot of arrests?" Popinga asked.

"You know, on Christmas Eve the cops aren't so tough. They'll take people down to the station but they let them go in the morning."

Jeanne Rozier came in. She was all dressed up, wearing a lot of perfume, flushed and sweating. It looked like she'd been dancing for hours. Thinking she'd just check in with him for a moment, she'd casually thrown her coat over her bare shoulders.

"Not having any trouble, are you? I heard there was a brawl."

"No, no—no trouble at all."

"I think Louis is going to take care of things. It seems like he hasn't made up his mind, but that's the way he always acts. Whatever you do, don't leave before I get back. You have no idea how hot it is in there. It's so packed that you can hardly lift your fork!"

She was taking him under her wing, it appeared, but at the same time she seemed a little anxious. He'd made an impression on her.

"You're not too bored?"

"Not at all."

She was already gone before he realized that she wasn't using the familiar with him anymore. That was satisfying! She understood! Unlike Pamela—that fat idiot bursting into mindless laughter.

He took out his notebook. On the page where he'd recorded Mother's opinions along with those of the train-station employee, Copenghem, and the man from the hotel, he made a new entry: "Jeanne Rozier certainly doesn't consider me insane!"

A slim woman resembling the one who'd come in before asked him to buy her a drink. He gave her five francs while making is clear she wasn't going to get anything else out of him!

He had carefully folded up all of his newspapers. Now he waited. That strange look of Frida's kept coming to mind. He wondered what was going to become of her.

It felt very hot, but even so he was sure that he was more coolly decisive and clear-sighted than he had ever been in his life. Would Mrs. Popinga follow through on her plan to work at a hotel in the Dutch East Indies?

He thought about getting in touch with Julius de Coster through the *Morning Post*. He'd place a small ad, simply: "How are you?"

He could do anything! He could be anything! He was through with presenting himself at all costs to the world as Kees Popinga, General Manager!

To think of the unheard-of lengths he'd gone to for so many years in order to stay in character, omitting nothing, not even under the most withering scrutiny! Which hadn't kept Copenghem from telling the press...

At any point he could have ordered a whole bottle of gin or brandy! Or taken the good-looking girl he'd just given five francs to to a hotel! Asked that jittery young man for cocaine! He could have...

"Waiter, some more mineral water!"

In protest against all those *could haves*! Because he was doing perfectly well as is, doing just fine; he felt drunk with his own lucidity. And in spite of that gigolo, Jeanne was sure to fall head over heels in love with him.

Around 4 AM she showed up, a little tipsy. She seemed surprised to see him. "Well, you're certainly a patient one!" she said with wonder.

Then, changing her tone: "Louis and the others aren't so sure. I've done what I can. Here's what they tell me: In a few minutes, they're going to leave the club, in two cars. They'll drive straight to the porte d'Italie. Do you know where that is?"

"No."

"Too bad—it's not going to work out then. Because they need you to take another car. They're going to stop and wait a moment at the porte d'Italie. As soon as you get there, flash your lights to let them know. After that, you just have to follow."

"Wait a second—do you take a right or a left to get to the porte d'Italie?"

"Neither—it's all the way across Paris."

"It doesn't matter. I'll ask a cop."

"Are you crazy? Or maybe you don't get it. We're talking about stealing a car—it belongs to some people who're eating at the club."

"I understand perfectly well. Still, it makes sense to ask the cops—that way they won't suspect me of anything."

"Go ahead! But I'm telling you Louis and his friends aren't going to wait long. And another thing, they don't want you to pick out anything too fancy. It has to be a car that won't stand out."

She was sitting right at his side, and for a moment he was sorry he hadn't taken advantage of her when he'd had the chance. She was worth it. How could he have failed to see?

"When will I see you next?" he asked in an undertone.

"I don't know. Depends on Louis. Look! They're leaving now."

He paid the bill and slipped his coat on, rolling up the newspapers to stuff in his pocket. Two cars pulled together into the heavy traffic that already filled the street.

"Aren't you going to say good-bye?"

"Yes—I like you a lot. You're—You're a fine woman."

Outside he could sense her watching him through the window, and he strolled off like a man with nothing more on his mind than getting home. He examined one car, then another. Finally he got into one and pressed the starter.

The car pulled smoothly away from the curb, and for a moment Popinga found himself following a big limousine full of women. He turned to wave good-bye to Jeanne Rozier, but the tobacconist's shop on the rue de Douai, where he had just spent Christmas Eve, was already out of sight.

5

In which Popinga is disappointed to find himself dressed in workclothes and traveling in circles in a garage; and how once again he demonstrates his independence.

IT WAS barely ten in the morning. The concierge had just woken up and the mail still lay in a pile in a corner of his booth, next to an untouched bottle of milk and a loaf of coarse bread. The streets were empty, the hopeless emptiness of the day after a holiday. Even the taxis were missing from their stands. There was nobody to be seen except for some church-goers on their way to mass, their noses red with the cold.

"What is it?" Jeanne Rozier asked. Her voice sounded thick. She'd been hearing the knocking for some time now without connecting it to her own door.

"Police!"

She woke up when she heard that. She searched around with her toes for her slippers. "Just a minute," she grumbled.

She was at home on the rue Fromentin. She'd slept alone; her green silk dress was lying over a chair; her stockings were strewn at the foot of the bed. She hadn't taken off her slip. She threw on a dressing gown before answering the door.

"What do you want?"

She thought she recognized the cop. He came into the

room, took off his hat, flipped on the light, and said straight out, "Lucas wants to see you. I'm under orders to bring you down to headquarters."

"The commissioner works on holidays?"

Jeanne Rozier may have been even more beautiful getting out of bed, all unkempt, than when she was dressed up to go out. Her red hair hid part of her face. In her unmade-up eyes there was a look of animal defiance.

She started getting dressed, without worrying about the cop, who was smoking a cigarette. He wasn't going to let her out of his sight.

"What's it like outside?"

"Freezing."

She dabbed some makeup on her face. Out on the street she asked, "Didn't you come by taxi?"

"No. There weren't any instructions."

"Okay. So I'll pay. I'm not going to take the bus halfway across Paris."

At headquarters, on the quai des Orfèvres, the corridors were empty, as were most of the offices. Without letting on, she had been considering all the angles. She was ready for the commissioner's questions.

Simply as a matter of policy he made her wait for a good fifteen minutes. Jeanne Rozier was too experienced to show any impatience.

"Well my dear, come in. Forgive me for having woken you up so early."

She sat next to a mahogany desk. She put her bag down and looked at Commissioner Lucas. He was bald and fatherly.

"Let's see, it's been quite a while since you've been here. The last time, if I remember correctly, was three years ago, on a little narcotics matter. So tell me—you're not with Louis anymore?"

The two first sentences were just for show, but the third shook her. "Who told you that?" she couldn't help but say.

"I don't remember really. Last night I was in Montmartre celebrating Christmas Eve, and someone told me that you'd taken up with a foreigner, a German or perhaps an Englishman."

"No kidding?"

"Which is why I wanted to see you. I'd hate to see you get into any trouble."

They talked like old friends. The commissioner paced the room, his fingers in his vest pockets. He'd offered her a cigarette, which she was smoking. She'd crossed her legs and fixed her gaze on a deserted embankment of the Seine. She could see a bridge with buses going back and forth.

"I think I know what you're talking about," she said after a moment's thought. "You're talking about the john from the day before yesterday, I bet."

Lucas pretended to be surprised.

"Oh, it was a john? I was told . . ."

"Who told you anything else? You must have been talking to Freddy, the headwaiter at Picratt's. They were about to close when the Dutch guy turned up, looking to have a good time. He called me over to his table, ordered champagne, and changed some Dutch bills to pay the check. We went to the rue Victor-Massé—it's where I always go because it's clean. We went to bed. He didn't touch me."

"Why not?"

"How do I know? In the morning I was sick of sleeping next to the fat soup-eater and left."

"Taking his money?"

"No. I woke him up and he gave me a thousand francs."

"For nothing?"

"That's not my fault."

"So you went home? Louis was there?"

She nodded.

"Indeed. And what has become of Louis? Is it true he wasn't there this morning?"

Her eyes flashed. "Why don't you tell me where he is then!" she muttered.

"You weren't together last night?"

"We were. We spent a nice quiet Christmas Eve with friends. I don't know who caught his eye, but what I do know is he slipped out and he didn't come home last night."

"He's got a lot of work, right?"

Her laugh was harsh.

"Why should he work? What would I be good for then?"

Lucas smiled and Jeanne Rozier let out a sigh. She wanted to know if he was done. They'd both played their roles to the best of their abilities. But they were still suspicious of each other. There was a lot to think about.

"Can I go back to bed now?"

"Of course, of course! Look, if you happen to see that Dutch guy again—"

"The first thing I'll do is slap his face," she said. "I can't stand creeps like him. If you think I don't know why you've been asking me questions for the last fifteen minutes—I read the papers, too! When I think about what happened to that showgirl in Amsterdam and how it could have happened to me..."

"You recognized him from his photograph?"

"I'd be lying if I said yes. He doesn't look like his picture. But when I guessed..."

"He didn't say anything? He didn't tell you any of his plans?"

"He asked me if I knew the Midi. And maybe Nice."

She was on her feet. The commissioner thanked her and within fifteen minutes she was back home again. She took a hot bath instead of going back to bed, after which she got dressed in ordinary street clothes to go out.

Around 12:30, she went into Mélie's, the favorite restaurant of the denizens of the rue Blanche. She sat down at a table and ordered a glass of port. She wasn't hungry.

"Louis?" the waiter asked. There was more to the question than appeared.

"I don't know—I suppose he'll come."

By three he still hadn't shown up. She left a message for him and went to see a movie nearby. It was five before he slipped into the seat beside her.

"You're late," she whispered.

"I had to go all the way to Poitiers."

"We need to talk. Careful—someone could be listening."

They left the theater for a crowded restaurant in the place Blanche.

"I got called into headquarters this morning by Lucas, the one who always treats me like I'm his daughter but is the worst of the lot. Where'd you leave our friend?"

"At Goin's. What a weirdo! Fernand was with me in the lead car, and he was sure he'd never make it to the port d'Italie. But he did. We'd just pulled up when we saw him signal. We were speeding all the way to Juvisy. We pulled into the garage and he drove in right behind us. It seemed like he'd been doing it all his life."

"What did he say?"

"Nothing at all. Goin was waiting with his mechanic. We all got to work and after an hour we were done. Rose made coffee. We left before dawn with the three cars, each of us in a different direction, except for that Dutch guy of yours, who's going to stay there until I figure out how much we can squeeze him for. He must have some money socked away."

"Be careful. The cops know I spent the night with him.

Lucas suspects something. That's why he wanted to see me at ten in the morning."

"Bad luck," Louis muttered. "I'll have to tell Goin."

"What if the phone's tapped?"

They looked like any stylish young couple sitting together. There was no sign of their feelings in their faces. Jeanne Rozier said, "We'll find some other way," as if that was enough. "Let's talk about it tomorrow. Tonight you'd better go somewhere where you'll be seen, a boxing match or a bike race, I don't know."

"Got it. Want to have dinner together?"

"No. I said you were running around with some girl. You'll have to try to find one."

She looked away and pinched his thigh: "Only, I'm telling you, don't get up to anything. If you do..."

———

After he'd heard Julius de Coster's revelations in the Little St. George, Kees had made up his mind that everything he'd believed in prior to that day was without basis in reality. So why was he surprised?

This was no ordinary garage, though at one time he might never have noticed. An ordinary garage isn't set a hundred yards off the highway, on a dead end, with two gas pumps sitting in the dark and doors that spring open automatically the moment somebody honks in a certain way. He knew that now.

And there were parts of more than a dozen cars scattered around a sort of empty lot. Not old cars—recent models. They'd been in accidents, and there was one that had been partly gutted by fire. In the glow of the headlights he'd had time to read the sign: GOIN AND BORET—AUTOMOTIVE ELEC-TRONICS SPECIALISTS.

He'd smoked a cigar as he watched the scene unfold after their arrival. There were two men waiting: a big guy, Goin, and a kid who could hardly have been the partner, Boret. Everyone called him Kiki. Goin was wearing brown overalls with wrenches sticking out of the pockets. No sooner had he and Louis shook hands than he was hard at work.

Everybody knew his job, you could tell that. The second car had been driven by a nice young fellow wearing a tux—like Louis and Fernand. Kees didn't catch his name.

The garage had a packed-earth floor and whitewashed walls, and apart from a small truck and some tools it was empty. A huge stove stood in one corner. Two powerful electric lamps shone down at an angle.

Louis pulled a suitcase out of the little truck while the others worked. He took off his clothes, like an actor switching costumes, and calmly changed into a brown suit and yellow tie. Then he put on a pair of overalls, in order to lend a hand.

Fernand and the other fellow did the same. Meanwhile, Goin worked with a blowtorch while Kiki removed the license plates from the cars.

"Rose isn't here?" Louis asked.

"She'll be down. I rang as soon as I heard you."

Kees saw a doorbell next to an inside door that must lead into the living quarters. A few minutes later a young woman came into the garage. She looked sleepy and she had clearly dressed in haste. She offered a friendly hello to everyone, including Kees. His presence didn't appear to surprise her.

"Nothing but three old wrecks! What kind of haul is that! You can tell it's Christmas."

"Make us some coffee, will you? Louis, you want to eat something?"

"No, thanks. I'm still stuffed."

Nobody was worried about the world outside. They were safe here. They worked, exchanging news and small talk.

"How's Jeanne?"

"She's the one who dug up our friend here, who's going to stay here until further orders. Be careful—he's pretty hot, and if he's caught . . ."

Within an hour the license plates had been switched and the serial numbers altered. There was a kitchen behind the garage, clean enough, and Rose served bread, butter, and sausages along with the coffee.

Louis sipped at his cup. "You," he said to Kees, "you're going to stay here and do what Goin tells you to do. Since you don't have any papers, don't even think about trying something smart. We'll be back for you. Got it?"

"I get it," Kees said with pleasure.

"We're off. Fernand will take the road to Reims. You, stay clear of Paris and try to unload that heap in Rouen. I'll head down to Orléans. Till tonight, boys! Till tonight, my pretty Rose!"

At first Kees found the new environment and these strange new people entertaining. Goin was nearly six feet tall and more muscled than the captain of the *Ocean III*. Now that his work was finished, he sipped at his coffee while carefully rolling a cigarette. Rose sat there looking drowsy, elbows on the table.

"You're foreign?"

"Dutch."

"If you don't want to get caught, better say you're English. A few of them live around here. Can you speak English? Do the cops have your description?"

Kees refilled his coffee, adding a lot of milk, while Goin went upstairs. He came back with a pair of old denim overalls like the ones he was wearing and a thick gray sweater.

"Here! Try these—they should fit. Rose will make a bed for

you in the little room behind ours. From what I hear, you'd better keep a low profile while you're waiting..."

Then Rose stood up. Probably she was going to make his bed. Goin was dozing off. His eyelids were fluttering as he sat motionless with his legs thrust out. A voice from upstairs cried, "You can come up!"

"Hear that? Go to bed—and good night."

The stairs were dark and narrow. Kees had to cross through Goin and Rose's room, which was a mess. He found himself in a smaller room where there was a camp bed, a table, and a shard of a mirror on the wall.

"Just use the sink in the hall to wash up. I hope you don't mind noise, because you're going to hear train whistles all day and all night long. We're right next to a train yard."

She shut the door behind her. Kees went to the window and pressed his face against it; in the dimming light, he could make out train tracks leading to infinity, train cars, whole trains, and at least ten locomotives, from which the smoke rose up spotless against the dirty sky.

He smiled, stretched, and sat down on the bed. Fifteen minutes later, without even bothering to undress, he was fast asleep.

He was still asleep when Jeanne Rozier was summoned to police headquarters in the morning, and he continued to slumber on as she sat down for lunch at the table at Mélie's. It was close to two when Rose, surprised by the long silence, cracked open the door, and yet Kees slept on.

Only at three did he wake up. He put on his new clothes—they made him look more heavy-set than he was—and crept down the dark stairs. There was a place set for him at one end of the kitchen table.

"Do you like rabbit?"

"Yes."

He liked everything.

"Where's your husband?"

"He's not my husband. He's my brother. He went to a soccer match ten miles away."

"The others haven't come back?"

"They never come back this way."

"And Jeanne Rozier? Does she sometimes show up?"

"Why would she? She's the boss's girl."

Without knowing why, he would have liked to see Jeanne again. It annoyed him to be apart from her. He ate the rabbit, dipping his bread into the thick gravy, and she kept coming to mind.

"Can I go for a walk?"

"Charles didn't say."

"Who's Charles?"

"My brother—Goin, if that suits you better."

Strange woman—more like a servant than anything. Her complexion was pale, almost lunar, and she was wearing much too much lipstick. She had on an orange silk dress that didn't suit her at all and her heels were too high.

"You'll stay at the garage all afternoon?"

"Someone has to be here. Tonight I'm going out dancing."

He wanted to go out and found himself in the streets of Juvisy, where everyone was wearing his Sunday best. He walked around in Goin's overalls and sweater with his hands stuck in his pockets and made up his mind to buy a pipe. He couldn't find anything that special, but he bought one anyway and filled it with gray tobacco. A bit later, he went into a café. The customers were playing pool.

Inside there was a slot machine. He'd never seen anything like it. Put in a franc, the wheels spun, and fruits popped up in different combinations that yielded two, four, eight, or sixteen francs—even the entire contents of the machine.

"I'd like fifty-one franc pieces, please."

Half an hour later he asked for another fifty; this was his kind of game. People were staring. They came over to watch him play. He'd taken the red notebook out of his pocket and was writing down every result.

At five o'clock, the air was blue with smoke and he was still playing. He paid no attention at all to what was going on around him. He'd begun to figure it out.

"So," he said to the barkeeper, "one out of every two coins goes into a special box for the owner."

"I don't know. It's not ours. The ones who installed it—they come and collect the money."

"How often?"

"Maybe once a week. Depends."

"How much does it bring in?"

"I don't know."

People were looking at him as he went on playing and making his complicated calculations. Meanwhile, his features never altered. Eight or twelve francs would tumble out, and without turning a hair he'd write down a number, then pocket them, and get back to the game.

Most of the customers worked on the railroad. Kees was still playing when he asked one of them, "Is there a main station here?"

"It's the biggest freight yard in Paris. They marshal the trains there. You know, if you keep that up, you're going to lose your shirt."

"I know."

"And you're not going to stop?"

He had to put down his pipe, which was getting in his way. He bought some cigars. He drank something he didn't know the name of but that most of the other customers were drinking. He liked the color.

What an odd Christmas! No one was going to church and

there wasn't a bell to be heard. Some people were playing cards at one of the tables. It was a family—father, mother, and two children. The father was playing with his friends, while the others looked on. From time to time, the children took a sip from his glass.

Popinga had completed his calculations.

Looking self-important, he approached the bartender. "Do you know how much a thing like this brings in? At least a hundred francs a day. Now suppose it costs five thousand francs—"

"What if someone hits the jackpot?" someone objected.

"It doesn't matter. Here, I'll explain . . ."

Two pages of his notebook were covered with calculations. They listened without understanding. After he left, someone asked, "Who was that?"

"I don't know. A foreigner, I'd say."

"Where's he work?"

"I don't know that, either. He blew two hundred francs on that machine. Strange."

"Must have been crazy."

A railroad worker concluded, "They're all like that—foreigners. That's why you can't understand a word they say."

Goin came back from his match and Rose went out dancing. The garage was closed. Goin, in slippers, was in the kitchen. He pulled out a newspaper and rolled a cigarette, looking like the calmest and happiest of men. Kees wrote notes in his book: "Profit on the three cars: at least thirty thousand francs. Repeat every week—which should be easy to do—and you bring in, for the year . . ."

Underneath, he wrote: "Would like to see Jeanne Rozier, find out why she arranged for me to come here."

He went to bed after that, though not before he'd spent some time contemplating the tracks in the night, the green and red lights, the darkened trains going by. And he couldn't stop thinking about Jeanne Rozier, imagining all sorts of intimacies, which, when he'd had the chance, had seemed unappealing. It was strange how differently he felt now.

The next day he rose at ten. There was a thin blanket of snow, not on the tracks, where it had melted, but between them and on the berm. Rose was in the kitchen, wearing a nightgown. He asked for her brother.

"He's gone to Paris."

Kiki was alone in the garage. He was trying to fix a starter, his tongue stuck out like a schoolboy.

"I want to go to Paris too," he said to Rose.

"My brother told me not to let you. He says you'll know why when you see the morning's paper."

"What's it say?"

"Don't know. I haven't read it."

Obviously she wasn't interested. She was frying onions in a pot on the stove. She didn't turn around when he unfolded the paper.

The case is sensitive, and we cannot report all the facts. But we can say that Christmas has not been a holiday for all: Commissioner Lucas has been hard at work. At any moment we can expect the arrest of the Amsterdam sex fiend, who...

Always, his madness! He underlined the words "sex fiend" in disgust. He had a funny smile on his face as he checked Rose out from behind. The nightgown made her big thighs all the more prominent.

Breaking news from Holland adds a further twist: the house of Julius de Coster has been taken into receivership. Did Kees Popinga take revenge on his boss when he learned that his life savings, which were entirely invested in the company, had been lost? Another explanation may lie in...

The words stuck in his mind: Commissioner Lucas. He got up, looked to see what was on the stove, and went out. The café was empty. He played the slot machine until noon, chatting with the bartender the whole time.

Back at the garage, Goin was eating lunch. He was wearing the suit he'd put on to go into the city and was almost unrecognizable.

He was furious. "At last!" he cried. "Are you out of your mind? Where have you been?"

"At a nice little café."

"Don't you have any idea what's going on? I saw the boss this morning. Yesterday a cop came for Jeanne Rozier. He dragged her out of bed and down to headquarters. If we don't end up in a heap of shit because of you, it'll be nothing but dumb luck!"

"What did she say?"

"Who?"

"Jean Rozier."

"I don't know. In any case, the boss absolutely forbids you to leave your room. Rose'll bring up your meals. You mustn't be seen around here for a few days—not until Louis gives the signal."

"You're not eating?" Rose said indifferently.

"I'm waiting for you to serve me."

"When he brought you here, I had no idea things were this serious. What the hell got into you? Are you nuts or something?"

"I don't know what you're talking about."

"Do you often get it—the urge to strangle women?"

"It was the first time. If she hadn't laughed . . ."

And he began to eat his beef stew and french fries.

"Listen, I want you to know that if you so much as touch my sister you're going to regret it. If I'd known how crazy you were—"

It didn't deserve a reply, Kees decided. Goin wasn't up to understanding. Better to say nothing and eat.

"And once you're in your room, don't think you're coming out again. It's enough that you went off and played the fool in every café in Juvisy. You didn't talk to anyone, at least, did you?"

"Yes."

Goin was raging, while Kees remained quite calm, enjoying himself. That was what was so funny!

"We'll have to see if the boss screwed up. I can't believe I thought you were someone worth helping!"

A real fight! Rose sat at a corner of the table like a good housekeeper, keeping an eye on the stove. Kiki was on the doorstep, balancing a plate on his knees.

Popinga preferred to keep his thoughts to himself. He appeared to be taking it all in, so Goin went on talking.

"The boss'll be back in three days at the latest. He has to go to Marseille tonight, but as soon as he returns . . ."

Popinga had already come to a decision. He finished his meal, wiped his mouth with his handkerchief, and said, "I'm going up to my room. Good night!"

They let him climb the stairs without saying a word, but before he reached the top Goin yelled out, "If you need something, just stamp on the floor three times. The kitchen's below you. Rose will hear."

Kees felt no desire to sleep. His window was set into the eaves, and with his elbows planted on the sill, he allowed his eyes to stray over the strange view, the snow-covered fields in the distance, the rails, buildings, and stacks of steel, all the disorderly contents of a large train yard, single train cars without engines, tiny faraway locomotives furiously going to and fro, whistles, shouts, a few trees that had escaped the general destruction, their branches scribbled on the frozen sky.

Kees remembered only one thing from all that had been said to him: Louis had left or would be leaving for Marseille.

Around four, sitting on his bed under the bare bulb, he reread: "The commissioner called a certain Jeanne R., 13, rue Fromentin, for questioning..."

It was cold and Kees had pulled the cotton bedspread up. The kitchen stovepipe passed through his room on its way to the roof, and he'd dragged his bed over to that side of the room. The trains let out their shrill blasts. Outside all the noises blended together, the high and low notes, the groaning engines, the occasional whine of a car speeding down the highway.

Louis would be leaving for Marseille, and that blank-faced Rose hadn't even looked at the paper to find out who he was. And Louis could curse all by himself... Unless he was already trying to sell him out...

But how much did it matter anyway? For now, the bulky sweater and overalls disguised the true Popinga—but he could shrug that off with contempt.

He was stronger than all the rest, even than Louis, or Jeanne Rozier. The whole gang was tied to the garage the same way Mother was tied to her house, and Claes to his patients and his mistress, Copenghem to the chess club he hoped to be president of...

And as to Popinga, he had no ties—not to a person, or an ideal, or anything at all. And he could prove it too.

6

The secrets of the stovepipe; Kees Popinga's second assault.

IT WAS pleasingly warm next to the stovepipe—you could almost feel the flames rising up within—and he might well have dozed off then if he hadn't been startled by the sound of the kitchen door opening below. Footsteps approached the oven followed by a tremendous racket that drowned out everything else. Somebody was stoking the fire and raking the coals. The noise was still going on when he overheard Goin asking, "Did you listen at the door? What's he up to?"

Rose's voice was testy in reply: "Can't say. He hasn't budged."

"Make me a cup of coffee, will you?"

"Sure. What are you fiddling with?"

"I'm trying to fix the alarm clock; it's broken."

Kees smiled. He could picture them together: Goin in his slippers, his brow furrowed and a burnt-out cigarette butt glued to his lip, busy taking apart and putting back together the alarm clock on the kitchen table. Judging by the noises, his sister was beginning to do the dishes.

"What do you make of him?"

The voices from below were muffled and all the more so because the conversation was being conducted without much passion or purpose, with long silences opening between the sentences. Sometimes it would be broken up by a train, leaving only bits and pieces behind.

Kees Popinga listened with eyes closed, relishing the gusts of heat.

"He's weird, that's what I think. I don't trust him. What did he do?"

"I just found out—strangled a showgirl in Amsterdam, after he offed an old man, or maybe."

Kees was utterly absorbed, but he had to stop to write down the word "offed" in the red notebook.

The water was boiling, and Rose was quick to grind the coffee. She set out a cup and the sugar bowl on the table.

"If I could only figure out where this flywheel goes . . ."

"Did you see Louis?"

"Yes. I had to find out his plan for our pal up there."

"What did he say?"

"You know how he is. He wants people to think he's got it all figured out, that he has a good reason for everything he does. Me, I've always said he makes it up along the way. He tried to tell me he's got the guy by the balls and can squeeze him for all he's worth. Yeah, I said, but he's got us, too."

"Drink your coffee while it's hot . . . You dropped a screw on the floor."

"But talk straight to Louis, and he gets angry. He yells at you that it's his business and let him take care of it. Go ahead, I told him. The cars are no problem. But I don't like having a nutcase like that Dutch guy in my house. Suppose he tries something with you."

"I'm not afraid of him."

"Not to mention, it could mean five years for all of us. What I think is that Jeanne fobbed the guy off on Louis. Louis can't say no, so without giving it any thought he agreed. There we go! Now let's see if it works."

The sound was so clear that Kees could practically see Goin winding up the rebuilt alarm clock.

"It's working?"

There was a crash; the garage mechanic had hurled the clock across the kitchen in a rage.

"You can go buy another one tomorrow. Did the paper come yet?"

"No."

"I told Louis what I thought. I said, with an opportunity like this, we need to make a deal with the cops. Hand over this sex fiend and it's pretty plain that they're going to look the other way when it comes to a lot of other things."

"What did he say?"

"Nothing. He'll think about it when he's back from Marseille."

"Do they have the death penalty in Holland?"

"I don't know. Why do you ask?"

"No reason."

A silence. Goin sounded annoyed: "If he were a human being like us, I wouldn't be talking this way. But you know what I'm trying to say. You saw for yourself the way he acts. I'm going out for the paper."

Kees Popinga hadn't moved. Outside the window, all he could see were a few lights high in the sky. Below, he heard Rose coming and going in her slippers, opening and closing the cupboards, arranging the china, feeding the stove.

Time stretched out. The newspaper must have been a pretext for Goin to pay a visit to the café and play cards. It was two hours before he got back; the table was set for dinner.

"Anyone come by?"

"No."

"Upstairs?"

"Must be asleep. I haven't heard him walking around."

"You know what I was thinking on my way back? That his kind's a lot more of a menace to society than people like us. Louis shot someone, on the boulevard Rochechouart, but he had to; the guy was trying to cheat him. In a case like that, at least you know where you stand. But this guy—do you have any idea what's going on in his head?"

"Probably nothing you'd want to know," muttered Rose.

"What can you do? I'm telling you, as far as I'm concerned, I don't want him in my house. Rabbit again! What do we have, a subscription?"

"It's left over from yesterday."

"We'll have to take some up."

"I'll do it after."

A few minutes later, Rose knocked on his door.

"Open up!" she said. "It's your dinner!"

Popinga was already on his feet. The way was clear, but with Rose carrying the tray, he managed to get between her and the door. He gave her a funny look.

"At least you're nice to me," he said.

Did he only want to scare her a little, or was it something more serious? He wasn't sure himself.

"Come on. Sit down. Stay a while."

She wasn't fazed. She turned and looked him up and down.

"Well what do you know!"

And she looked him straight in the eyes. He smiled nervously. His hands were trembling.

"You don't think I'm a showgirl, do you? You'd be better off eating up and going to bed!"

She didn't lose her temper. Through sheer presence of mind, she forced him to get out of her way. She turned at the door.

"When you're done, just leave the tray outside."

Seconds later, Popinga was pressing his cheek to the stovepipe. He heard the kitchen door open and close. A chair scraped the floor, and Rose sat down. A silence. The clink of a bottle against a glass.

"Was he asleep?"

"I guess."

"He didn't say anything?"

"What's he supposed to say?"

"I thought I heard you talking."

"I told him to leave the tray outside the door when he was done."

"You have to agree—Louis is being careless. If Lucas summoned Jeanne to headquarters, he's got to have some idea. They must be watching Jeanne—Louis, too. I wonder if the cops knew I was going to see him today. What if I was followed?"

"You want to turn him in?"

"What I'm saying is, apart from Louis..."

He must have gone back to his newspaper, because for a long time there was nothing to hear. Finally Goin let out a sigh: "How about turning in? Nothing coming in tonight. I'm going to close the garage."

Popinga did as instructed: he put the tray outside the door, and carefully shut it behind him. Then he removed the clothes that Goin had given him and put on his own gray suit. He slipped his money and his red notebook into the pockets.

He had no sense of impatience. He lay under the covers on the bed and waited. Next door brother and sister undressed quietly, with few words, moving some things around now and then. They'd been in the country and born poor, and ever since childhood they'd been accustomed to sleeping five or six to a room.

"Night, Rose."

"Night!"

"I'm not saying I can tell the future. You don't see it the way I do, I know. But I'm right—you'll see!"

"Maybe," she answered—either resigned or half asleep.

Popinga waited fifteen minutes, then half an hour. He got up and walked to the window without a sound. It was snowing. For a moment, he was worried: What would happen when he opened the window? The noise from the train yard would come bursting into the house. Wouldn't the two of them wake up?

But he knew it would go fast. Some six feet under the window there was a small truck with a tarpaulin stretched out over the top. Popinga dangled and dropped. It took him no time at all to find his way to a vacant lot behind the garage, leaving his footprints in the light dusting of snow.

What time was it, he wondered—but his watch was gone; Goin must have taken it. He got his bearings, reached Juvisy, and passed the café with the slot machine. He almost went in, to let them see him in his own gray suit and overcoat, wearing a collar and tie.

He learned the time at the station: 10:40. He went in and politely asked the clerk when the next train left for Paris.

"Twelve minutes," he was told.

Waiting on the platform, he was overwhelmed with a sense of relief. Not that he was the least bit afraid, any more than he'd been at the garage! He hadn't felt fear from the moment he'd left Groningen. But in Juvisy, he'd come close to losing everything he'd gained from his escape.

It was almost like he'd been taken prisoner—with Louis and Goin's sister Rose standing in for Mme Popinga and Julius de Coster.

And they didn't understand him any better than the people back home. What was the word Goin had used? He checked his notebook: "Offed"!

They thought he'd *offed* Julius de Coster. They thought he was a *nutcase*.

Even worse: lying on the cot listening to the noises below, he'd almost thought for a moment that he was back home in

Groningen—up in his room, overhearing his wife gossiping with the maid. They talked back and forth to each other with the same calm certainty as Goin and Rose; they also passed judgment on people and things as if the whole world depended on it.

But Goin was probably right about Louis: he was a kid who'd gotten mixed up in a grown-up game. He didn't really know what he was doing.

Popinga felt stronger than ever. He paced the platform, examining the tourist posters and smoking a cigar. He was miles ahead of loudmouths and boasters like Louis, Goin, and Julius de Coster!

He bought a newspaper. He was sure that he'd find something concerning him inside. Maybe they'd print his picture again. He was wanted by the police. People trembled at the thought that the notorious Amsterdam sex fiend might be stalking them.

And as to him, he'd calmly come out of hiding, bought a second-class ticket, and was now waiting for a train to Paris, the very place where Commissioner Lucas was conducting his investigation.

Didn't that prove that he was stronger and smarter than the whole lot of them? He'd do better yet: he would go see Jeanne Rozier. Why? Because it was dangerous, because it was the one thing he absolutely shouldn't do.

But he needed to see her. There were some things they needed to settle.

The train pulled into the station and he happened to end up in a compartment with two women from the country who were dressed in black. They were going on about village news: sick neighbors, recent deaths.

He sat quietly in his corner, looking at them. He had a wild impulse to burst out: "Allow me to introduce myself—Kees Popinga, the Amsterdam sex fiend!"

He didn't do it. But he kept thinking about it. He took an evil pleasure imagining the scene that would inevitably follow. And yet in Paris he was the one who stood in line to get their bags. A real gentleman. "At your service," he murmured, though he couldn't suppress an ironic smile.

Finally, this is what he wanted: he wanted to be the only one, absolutely the only one, to know what he knew. He alone could identify Kees Popinga. He alone could move freely through the crowd while others brushed by, clueless, with all their different stupid ideas about who he was.

The two women, for example, thought he was the kind of gentleman you don't often encounter nowadays. And Rose? Well, she hadn't said just what she thought, but with her lack of imagination she had to hate him.

He was happy to be back in Paris. He enjoyed the buses and taxis, the people running pointlessly in every direction with God knows what on their minds. As for him, he had time to kill. Picratt's never closed before three or four in the morning. Even if Jeanne Rozier had gone out on her own, she wouldn't be home until close to a quarter past three.

It was strange, really strange, that Kees hadn't taken advantage of her when he'd had the opportunity. In a bed he'd paid for, too! And now he could think of nothing else.

But it was different. Now that she knew, he needed to impose himself on her; he needed to feel her fear. She was too smart to push him away like that stupid Rose.

He had nothing to do, so he went up to a cop and asked him for directions to the quai des Orfèvres. That was a good question! In all the newspaper stories about him, they brought up the quai des Orfèvres and Commissioner Lucas. Kees was excited when he reached the place and made out the word "Police" above a dimly lit door. What he really wanted was to get a glimpse of the commissioner himself, but that wouldn't be easy.

So for a time, he sat on a wall above the Seine, contentedly observing three windows on the second floor where the lights were still burning. Two vans and a radio car waited in the courtyard beyond the big ornamental gate.

He was sorry to leave. He'd longed to go in, to see things up close. And no sooner had he reached the place Saint-Michel than he turned back. Once again he stopped a cop, to find out how to get to Montmartre. He would have stopped the cop even if he'd known the way. It was a pleasure to speak with an officer of the law. "He doesn't have any idea," Kees thought to himself.

He couldn't go on walking until three in the morning, so he stopped along the way at cafés. A few people would be standing around a horseshoe-shaped counter, their lives suspended. Some dreamed as they drank their coffees. Others, with their elbows on the counter, stood empty-eyed over empty drinks. Nothing but magic, it seemed, would bring them back to life. There was a little girl carrying a basket of violets who reminded him of Christmas Eve—when Jeanne Rozier had come in twice to check up on him at the tobacconist's on the rue de Douai.

Goin must have been right: Jeanne had convinced Louis to take him in. But why? Because he'd made an impression on her? Because he didn't act like a typical john? Or because she was curious when she'd found out what he'd done?

Popinga would never believe that she might have felt sorry for him. Jeanne Rozier wasn't the kind of woman to take pity on someone, and he didn't want pity anyway.

"Another hour to go!" he realized. He grew impatient.

He thought about her more and more as the hour approached. He tried to imagine what was going to happen. He'd had nothing but mineral water to drink up till then, but now he started in on brandy. Soon there was a flush to his cheeks.

Two AM. He examined himself in the mirror of a café on the

boulevard des Batignolles. "Nobody has any idea what's going to happen," he thought, "not even me! Not even Jeanne, who just wants to go home! Louis is in Marseille. Goin and his sister are asleep in their room, imagining I'm in the other room. Nobody knows anything."

He asked for a paper. He had to flip to the fifth page before he found a few lines about himself. How annoying! And it was the same old song: "Commissioner Lucas continues his investigation of the Amsterdam crime. He believes that Popinga will soon be arrested."

Commissioner Lucas—there was another one who thought he was smart but didn't know a thing! But maybe he was trying to frighten Kees. He could have planted the story, after all.

So the commissioner thought he had all the answers! Right away Kees decided to put him to the test. He asked a cop how to get to the rue Fromentin and walked the length of the street three times. He checked out every hiding place along the way. One thing he knew—there weren't any cops lying in wait around number thirteen.

Which meant no one had guessed that he'd be paying a visit there that night. Which meant that Lucas really didn't understand a thing. And that Popinga was way ahead of them all.

What would the commissioner do if something happened tonight? What would the papers say, after parroting all his promises?

In any case, Kees had to take action. Because the more he took action, the more they'd be at a loss, coming up with new hypotheses—contradictory hypotheses—and ending up in a state of utter confusion.

What was holding him back? What was there to prevent him, not all that long ago, from attacking those two women on the train, from pulling the emergency cord and calmly leaving the train while everyone rushed back and forth in the corridor?

He had no trouble finding Picratt's, where he'd spent his first few hours in Paris, and he walked around the neighborhood, waiting for it to close. All in all, he'd still been in the dark when he'd first arrived. There hadn't been time to think things over. Now he was filled with something close to pity at the thought of the fellow who'd left the train at the Gare du Nord and rushed off to order champagne and chat up some girl.

Two women emerged from the club—hostesses like Jeanne. She wasn't one of them, though.

He was annoyed when he realized that she might come out with a client. Then everything would have to be delayed until later—maybe tomorrow.

But no! Here she came! She was in her squirrel-fur coat, with a bouquet of violets hanging down from one hand. Her high heels tapped loudly on the sidewalk.

She was shivering and walking quickly, hugging the houses, not looking back. It seemed like she must make the same walk at the same time every day.

Kees followed her from across the street. She wouldn't escape.

He had a minor scare, however, when she walked into one of the few cafés that were still open. He watched through the window. He was amazed to see her order a coffee into which she dunked a croissant.

No one had asked her out to dinner! She ate with the same blank expression he'd noticed earlier on faces in the other cafés. She rummaged in her bag, paid, and left without wasting time.

He waited as she rang to be let in; the door clicked open, and he appeared without a word. She jumped. She didn't open her lips, didn't say anything, but he could see the fear in her green eyes. Then she shrugged. She flattened herself against the doorway to let him pass.

Jeanne operated the elevator. It was so narrow that they were squeezing against each other. She sent it back down and looked for her key in her bag. Finally she stammered, "What are you going to tell Louis?"

He just smiled. She was taken aback. Because she knew that he knew, that he'd guessed her trick. When they were inside the apartment Kees said in an undertone, "Louis is in Marseille."

"Goin told you that?"

"No."

She shut the door and turned on the light in the entryway. There were three rooms and a bathroom in the apartment; it was old-fashioned, stuffy, with rugs everywhere and endless knickknacks. A pair of slippers lay on the floor. There was a sandwich and a half-empty bottle of wine on the table.

"Why'd you come here?"

Yes, her eyes were green—just as he remembered. Fear made them greener yet.

"I could have summoned the concierge."

"What for?"

He removed his coat as if to make himself at home. He took a swig of some wine from the bottle and opened the bedroom door. There was a telephone on the night table—he'd have to keep an eye on that. Jeanne Rozier had seen him look. She could have guessed his thoughts.

He was playing with her, and he was enjoying it. She had keen intuitions; she kept her cool. Only little things gave her away.

"You're not going to undress?" he said, taking off his tie and collar.

She still had her squirrel-fur coat on. Now she let it fall from her shoulders. It was a gesture of resignation.

"As soon as I heard Louis was in Marseille, I decided I'd better seize my chance. Who's the person in the picture over the bed?"

"My father."

"A good-looking man. What an amazing mustache!"

And he sat down on a small old-fashioned sofa to pull off his shoes. Jeanne Rozier, however, kept her clothes on. She took a few steps around the room and then stopped in the middle. "I hope you're not counting on staying here," she said.

"Yes, at least till tomorrow."

"I'm sorry—that won't be possible."

She had guts. And yet she couldn't keep her eyes from wandering toward the telephone. He didn't bother to reply. He just laughed and pulled off his other shoe.

"Did you hear what I said?"

"I heard, but it doesn't matter, does it? You forget—we've already shared a bed. I was totally exhausted that night. Not to mention I didn't know you yet. I've been sorry ever since."

He remained seated, pleased with himself. He had a slight fever, and it gave his voice an added resonance.

"Listen," she said, "I didn't want to make a scene downstairs, waking up the concierge and the other tenants. I know the risks you're running. But you're going to get dressed again, right now! You're going to get out of here! I have to believe that you're not so crazy that you'd think I'd be willing to do anything like that now that..."

"Now that what?"

"Nothing!"

"Now that you know? Tell me! Now that you know what happened to Pamela? Answer me! I promise you all this gives me enormous pleasure. For three days I've been trying to figure out what's on your mind."

"You shouldn't have gone to so much trouble."

"For three days I've been telling myself: 'This one is smarter than the rest.'"

"Maybe so, but you're getting out of here anyway."

"And if I don't?"

He was standing in his socks, with his collar buttoned over his Adam's apple.

"Too bad for you."

She'd taken a small pistol with a mother-of-pearl handle out of a side table. She hadn't aimed it at him, but she was holding it in her hand in a way that was hardly reassuring.

"You'd shoot?"

"I don't know. Probably."

"Why? I mean, why don't you want to now—that's what I'm asking. It was me who didn't before."

"I'm begging you—get out!"

She was preparing to steal over to the phone. But she was clumsy; she showed her fear even as she struggled to hide it. And maybe that was what made Kees do it—maybe that was what pushed him over the edge. Still, he didn't lose his acting skills.

"Listen, Jeanne," he whimpered, hanging his head, "you're being mean. You're the only one who understands me and yet..."

"Not a step closer."

"I'm not coming any closer. I'm begging you to listen to me, to answer me. I know Goin and his sister wanted to turn me over to the police."

"Who told you that?" she replied angrily.

"I heard them talking about it. I also know that Louis was expecting to pick up the reward."

"That's not true!"

"Yes it is! He probably didn't tell you, but he told Goin, and Goin told his sister. I heard them talking. I climbed out the window and I came here."

She must have been surprised—she'd let down her guard a little. Her eyes were glued to the rug; she was thinking.

Without any change in expression, he continued: "The gun—that's what proves you knew about it. You'd turn me in too."

"No!"

She raised her head sharply. You could tell she meant it.

"So what's it for?"

"Don't you understand?"

"Are you telling me you're frightened?"

"No!"

"So why?"

"Nothing!"

Now he was three steps closer. Two more, and he'd be on top of her. The die was cast, the wheels had been set in motion, even if he had no idea what he intended to do.

"You have to understand—"

"Shut up!"

"If she hadn't been so stupid—"

"Shut up, I'm telling you!"

She made an impatient gesture, and for a second the pistol pointed away. Kees seized his chance with total assurance. He leaped on her in a flash, knocking her back onto the bed and grabbing the weapon out of her hand. At the same time, he covered her face with a pillow to keep her from crying out. He pressed down as hard as he could.

"Promise you won't scream!"

She fought. She was strong. The pillow slipped off and then he hit her on the head with the butt of the pistol, once, twice, three times, perhaps many more, he didn't know and he didn't care. He was just waiting for her to stop moving.

He put on his shoes after washing off the blood he'd noticed on his hands. He'd been calm after Pamela, and he was calm now, but there was something oppressive about this feeling of calm, even a certain regret. The proof was that when he was washed and dressed he paused for a moment by the bed. He touched Jeanne's hair and murmured, "How sad!"

And it wasn't until he reached the staircase that he was able to shrug it off. He consoled himself with the thought: "Well, at least that's over."

What was over? Only he knew what he meant, that much was for sure, even if he couldn't explain it. It was everything— everything that could have reconnected him to other people and their lives. From now on he was on his own. He was completely alone and alone against the whole world.

He couldn't open the door in the lobby, and for an instant he panicked. He wasn't used to Paris—he had no idea how things worked—and he lost it. He was afraid, his forehead covered with sweat.

For a moment he thought of climbing back upstairs to the second floor: he'd wait until morning, when the other tenants left for the day. But then, as luck would have it, somebody rang to be let in. The door opened; a couple entered. They turned in astonishment at the sight of his fleeing shadow.

More people who would talk about him tomorrow to the police!

Montmartre was quiet. All the neon signs were dark. Now and then a taxi slowed down to see if he wanted a ride.

Why take a taxi? He didn't even know where he was going.

Something was tormenting him, though: the image of Jeanne Rozier; it could be a while before she regained her senses and maybe she . . .

Too bad! He flagged down the next taxi. He had a hard time explaining what he wanted.

"Yes, that's it! Go to 13, rue de la Fromentin. You'll go up to the fourth floor, to Mme Jeanne Rozier's. She's waiting for a taxi to take her to the train station immediately. Here's twenty francs in advance."

The driver seemed suspicious.

"Are you sure this lady—"

"I'm telling you, she's waiting!"

The driver shrugged and started the car. Popinga strode off toward the center of town. Let the hunt begin now or later—it made no difference to him. He'd escape anyway.

Would Jeanne Rozier help the police out by giving them his exact description? He was dying to know. It didn't make sense, but something told him she wouldn't.

He was tired. He wanted to sleep for twelve hours, maybe a whole twenty-four, the way he had the other day.

If he went to a hotel, he'd have to fill out a form. Perhaps they'd ask him for his papers. But hadn't Jeanne taught him the trick?

He strode along until he saw a girl who, late as it was, was still out. He made a sign and followed her. In the room, he was careful to slide his money under the pillow.

"You're a foreigner?"

"Who's to say? What I need is sleep! Here's a hundred francs—just leave me alone!"

He fell asleep and dreamed that he was Kees Popinga again. Mother was silently getting dressed. She looked at herself in the mirror and popped a little pimple. Below, the maid was making a racket in the kitchen. Except it was Rose. A little later he went downstairs and crept up on her from behind. She said, "When I come back into the kitchen, you'll be gone!"

A voice whispered, "Be careful! There's sugar in the box marked 'Salt.' It tastes awful in oxtail soup."

He struggled to recognize the voice, and all of a sudden it dawned on him: it was Jeanne Rozier. Now he was in his socks, with his collar off, standing in the middle of his kitchen. The house was filled with guests. She was laughing. She seemed friendly but she was making fun of him: "Get dressed—quick! Don't you realize they'll recognize you?"

7

How Kees Popinga makes himself at home on the run, and how he feels duty-bound to assist the French police in their investigation.

YOU START small, with a detail, even a trivial one. Then, without expecting it, you stumble on the great idea.

That morning, when he looked at himself in the mirror—a task he'd always taken very seriously—Popinga realized he hadn't shaved since leaving Holland. His beard wasn't all that heavy, but it didn't make him look attractive either.

He turned toward the bed. He hardly recognized the woman who was sitting there. She was pulling on her stockings.

"When you're ready, go get me a razor, shaving brush, and some shaving soap. And a toothbrush as well."

He'd given her the money up front, and there wasn't really any reason for her to come back, but she was trustworthy. When she returned she insisted on showing him exactly how much she had spent. She didn't know whether she should stay or go, and she was afraid to ask, so she sat down on the bed again and watched him shave.

The hotel was on one of the streets leading off the faubourg Montmartre, and it was a lot seedier than the one on the rue Victor-Massé. The same difference could be discerned between

Jeanne Rozier and the woman on the bed. Nobody would be giving her four stars.

Then again, she was going out of her way to please him. Kees didn't know her name, but she was doing what she could to figure him out. He could tell because she heaved a sigh and asked, "You're unhappy, aren't you? I bet somebody broke your heart."

She sounded like a fortune-teller—confident but cautious.

"Why do you say that?" he replied. There was lather all over one of his cheeks.

"Because I think it's fair to say I know something about men. How old do you think I am? . . . Listen, sweetheart, I'm thirty-eight. I know I don't look it . . . And I've seen a lot of guys like you, right, who pick you up and then don't do a thing. And usually at some point they just start talking, talking and talking, spilling the beans. It's good for us, though. We listen to the whole story, and it doesn't go any further."

It was almost like family: Kees, with his flabby bare chest and trailing suspenders; the woman rattling off sweet nothings while she waited for him to get ready. The really funny thing was that, according to her, he was a sad sack. It was another of those new personalities people kept finding for him; he'd have to remember to make a note of it. Then at some point he just stopped listening.

The razor had started a new train of thought. For a while he wondered if he shouldn't buy a suitcase to keep his things in.

Because if he showed up late without any bags, it might attract attention at a real hotel. With a suitcase, he could pass for a traveling salesman. But what was he going to do with it the rest of the day? Store it in a locker at the train station? Drop it off at a café?

But then he'd decided, in any case, that he wasn't going to

sleep in the same place twice. He knew what got people caught was someone noticing some detail or other that didn't quite fit in.

"Forget the suitcase!" he muttered. He carefully washed his razor and wrapped it up in a bit of newspaper.

Not to mention there was the risk he'd end up being "the man with the suitcase." Just that one everyday object would be enough to betray him.

He thought of things like that, which was why he was superior to the sort of people you read about in the newspapers—thieves, murderers, escaped convicts. He thought about things—the way he used to attend to business for Julius de Coster and Son—coolly, totally detached, as if he had no personal stake in the matter.

He was looking for the answer, the right one—nothing less. "Do you have to show papers at a place like this?" he asked abruptly.

"Never. Sometimes they need a name just to fill out the form. And every few months or so, the police show up in the middle of the night and drag everybody out of bed. That's mostly when somebody important from abroad is coming through, in case of assassination."

Kees wrapped up the shaving brush and soap and the toothbrush and distributed them among his pockets. With the red notebook and the pencil, that was the sum of his possessions.

It really was convenient! He could go wherever he wanted, sleep every night in a different hotel—or even a different part of the city. Of course there were those raids the woman had mentioned, but he figured the odds at about a hundred to one.

"Want to take me to lunch?" she asked.

"Not really."

"I'm not going to insist. I just said it to make you happy. So you don't need me anymore?"

"No."

They split up on the sidewalk—it was a street full of fruit carts. Popinga no longer had his watch, but a clock at the corner said it was 12:15.

He liked it around here. The neighborhood was swarming with all kinds of people; there were cafés everywhere, all of them packed.

He calculated that the three thousand francs he had left would last about a month. By that time, he'd have found some way to get more money.

Just like that he turned stingy. Before he'd been a spendthrift. Now, however, his money carried a special significance —like the razor in his pocket, like the suitcase he didn't have, like all the little details of the survival strategy he was busy working out.

Which is how he came to be standing for nearly an hour in front of the map of Paris at an entrance to the Métro. His memory for topography was remarkable. The various neighborhoods, the major arteries, the grand boulevards: they all fell into place in his mind precisely as they appeared on the map. When he set off again, he knew his way around Paris—no need to ask for further directions.

He didn't feel like having lunch, but stopped in a café where he ate some croissants and drank two big glasses of milk. He reached the grand boulevards in time to buy the afternoon papers, which had just come out.

Jeanne Rozier and her fate had been on his mind all morning, even if he'd pretended otherwise. Now he turned the pages of the papers eagerly. He was amazed, irritated, and finally outraged when he failed to find a single line about the subject. There wasn't anything about him, either. The story of Pamela appeared to be completely forgotten. Instead everybody was carrying on about some mysterious event on the Paris–Basel express.

Obviously, if Jeanne Rozier were dead, the newspapers would already have been told. So . . .

Unless . . . Maybe it was a trap. Maybe not. Who knew? Maybe the police had hushed things up hoping he'd do something stupid. If he'd just gotten a glimpse of this Commissioner Lucas—even if only through a window!—he would have had something to go by. At the very least he could have figured out the kind of man he was and what kind of tricks he might get up to.

But so what! There was one thing he could do that wasn't too risky: Jeanne had a telephone on her night table.

He went into a restaurant and looked up her number. The operator connected him and a strange voice answered. It sounded like a middle-aged woman.

"Hello—is Mlle Rozier there?"

"Who's calling?"

"Tell her it's a friend."

So she wasn't dead. There was a silence. "Hello! Would you like to leave a message? Mlle Rozier is indisposed. She can't come to the phone."

"Is it serious?"

"Not very serious, no, but—"

That was enough! He hung up and returned to his seat in the main room of the restaurant. Some fifteen minutes later he summoned the waiter. He asked for some writing paper.

He was in a lousy mood. He thought about what to say for a long time. Finally he wrote in firm, careful letters:

To the Commissioner of Police,

    I must inform you of a new development last night that is of some importance to the Popinga case. Perhaps you would be interested in going to the residence of Mlle Rozier in the rue Fromentin and asking her under what circumstances she came to be in the state in which you will discover her.

He hesitated, wondering if he should go on. With quiet satisfaction he thought of Goin and, especially, of Goin's sister. He continued:

Also this is an opportunity for me to collaborate further with the French police, who are sufficiently interested in me that I would like to look after their interests in turn.

You will soon have a chance to lay hands on a gang of car thieves that operates on a very large scale. Among other things, on Christmas Eve members of this gang stole three cars in the Montmartre quarter alone.

Set an ambush for them at night around the garage of Goin and Boret in Juvisy. Don't bother to go tonight or tomorrow either. Nothing is going to happen, since the leader is in Marseille. Begin surveillance on the following nights. It would surprise me very much if you do not succeed before the New Year.

I am very truly yours,
Kees Popinga

He read his letter over and was satisfied. He sealed it in an envelope and addressed it before calling the waiter.

"Tell me—if I send a letter now, when will it be delivered?"

"To a Paris address? Tomorrow morning. But send it express and it'll get there in less than two hours."

He was always learning something new. He sent the letter express and left the neighborhood. He'd deliberately used the restaurant stationery.

It was four in the afternoon. It was pretty cold, and a fine mist was gathering around the gaslights. He kept walking and eventually encountered the Seine exactly where he'd expected to—at the Pont-Neuf. He crossed the bridge.

He wasn't walking at random. He had a precise destination in mind. Now that he'd taken care of business, he wanted to play some chess.

Where would a newcomer in Groningen go to play chess? The big student café near the university.

The same must be true in Paris. Kees made his way to the Latin Quarter and then to the main street there, the boulevard Saint-Michel. It could be a mistake—the neighborhood didn't seem anything like the quiet town of Groningen—but he went ahead anyway.

He peered through the windows of a dozen cafés: no one was playing any games and the people inside didn't seem to be planning on staying long.

But across the boulevard, on the second floor of a restaurant, he saw people with billiard sticks silhouetted against the blinds.

He was proud of himself—he felt like he'd already won a game—and a moment later, he was prouder yet. He climbed up to the second floor of the place in question and entered a bare, smoke-filled room with a dozen pool tables lit by lamps with green shades. All around there were tables where people were playing backgammon, cards, and chess.

With the same solemn formality that he displayed at his own Dutch club, Kees removed his heavy overcoat and went to the bathroom to wash his hands. After cleaning his nails and running a comb through his hair, he seated himself by a couple of young chess players. He ordered a half-pint of beer and lit a cigar.

Too bad he'd decided never to go to the same place twice—otherwise he would have spent every afternoon here. There were no women—that alone was enough to make him happy. Most of the young people—students—had taken off their jackets to play billiards.

One of the chess players was a Japanese fellow with tortoiseshell glasses. The other was a big blond kid whose red face revealed his every feeling.

Kees pulled his gold-rimmed glasses from his pocket—once again as in Groningen—and cleaned them carefully before putting them on. Then the minutes ran together as he abandoned himself to the contemplation of the chessboard. Every piece fell into place in his mind just as the whole map of Paris had earlier.

Beer mingled with cigar smoke and sawdust—even the smell of the room reminded him of the chess club in Groningen. Even the behavior of the waiter, who interrupted his rounds to stand behind the players and surreptitiously watch their games!

Kees could sit without moving for hours in such circumstances, his legs crossed, while the ash on his cigar grew ever longer.

Only when the game was almost over did he bother to reach out and tap the ash free. The Japanese guy was looking particularly unhappy; he had been staring at the board for some ten minutes without making up his mind what to do. "You win in two moves, don't you?" Kees said quickly.

The Asian gave him an astonished look. He seemed to feel worse, if anything, given that he'd been sure he was going to lose. And his opponent was no less surprised. He couldn't see any way for someone to checkmate him. He was sure to win.

A silence fell. The Japanese guy reached out toward his rook, jerking it back as if it were red hot. Then he looked to Popinga for advice. The blond kid studied the positions again. He sighed and said, "I absolutely don't see how..."

"Allow me?"

The Asian nodded yes. The other waited skeptically.

"I move the knight here—what do you do?"

Without thinking, the blond kid said, "Take it with my rook."

"Excellent! I move my queen forward two squares. What do you do now?"

This time the young man was at a loss; he was confused for a moment. Then he moved his king back one square.

"There you go! So I move my queen forward one square—check and mate! Nothing to it, you know."

In such cases he always tried to look modest, but his face was glowing with satisfaction. The young men were so shocked that they didn't even think about a new game.

But the Japanese guy forced himself to think the position through. Finally, he said, "Do you want to play?"

"You can have my place," the other said.

"No, no! If you like, I'll play you both at the same time. Each of you take a chessboard."

He was rubbing his hands together in a way that made them appear to their full advantage. They were a little fleshy, yes, but white, shapely, and remarkably soft.

"Waiter! Another chess set!"

The letter wouldn't have reached Lucas yet, but by the time the two games were over it would be in his hands. No doubt he'd make his way as fast as he could to the rue Fromentin.

The young men were completely daunted. The discomfort was increased because Popinga, on the banquette across from them, was taking malicious pleasure in following a game of billiards from a distance at the same time.

He played without hesitation on both boards. His opponents took their time, especially the Asian, who was determined to win.

In the meantime, Popinga found himself wondering how he could get his hands on a list of all the cafés where people played chess.

Studying the map of Paris, he'd made a discovery that led him to think there must be quite a few. In Groningen, as in most towns, there was a single central square, like the pit of a fruit, which was surrounded on all sides by houses.

Kees had observed that Paris had many centers. And every neighborhood must have its nucleus with cafés, movie theaters, dance halls, busy streets.

Someone who lived in Grenelle wouldn't go to the boulevard Saint-Michel to play chess any more than someone from around the parc Montsouris. So all he had to do was visit the different parts of town.

"I beg your pardon," he said, with an air of confusion. "Why don't you go ahead and take back your bishop—if you don't, it'll be check from my queen."

It was the blond kid. He blushed and stammered, "Well, the move's been made."

"No, no—I beg you!"

Meanwhile the Japanese guy was casting sidelong glances at his companion's game. He didn't want to make the same mistakes.

"What are you both studying?"

"Medicine," said the Asian.

The blond kid hoped to be a dentist. That seemed right up his alley.

In spite of his intense concentration, the Asian was the first to lose. His friend concentrated even harder after that. Still, he only lasted a few minutes.

"What can I get you?" The kid dutifully offered.

"Nothing. The round's on me."

"But we lost."

He insisted on buying them drinks. Lighting a fresh cigar, he leaned back against the banquette.

"The essential thing, you see, is to have the whole game in your head, never forgetting that the bishop's protecting the queen, the queen the knight..."

And he'd almost gone right on saying "that Louis, forewarned by Jeanne Rozier, must already be on the train from Marseille. That at this very moment Commissioner Lucas is arriving at the rue Fromentin, where Jeanne is wondering what he wants. That in Juvisy, Goin is scared to pick up the phone because of the trouble he might find himself in, and that Rose..."

He continued: "And, of course, you must make a close study of any tricks your opponent gets up to while avoiding them yourself. If I'd played a trick, I might have beaten one of you, but then the other would have seen what I was up to and could have gotten the better of me."

He really was very pleased with himself. So much so that he stayed on at the café even after the two young men thanked him and departed. With a cigar stuck between his lips and his thumbs hooked in his vest pockets, he followed a game of billiards from afar, resisting the temptation to join in.

Because he was as good at billiards as he was at chess, he could have taken the stick from one of the players and scored a good fifty points in a row.

His opponents at chess had been unaware of the mirrors across the room from him. The room was dimly lit, the air hazy with pipe and cigarette smoke. His reflection was blurred, even mysterious, and he observed it with pleasure, both lips pulling on his cigar.

It was six in the evening, according to the clock in its blue-green enamel frame. To while away the hours, he took out his notebook. He thought for a long time before writing.

He realized that, even if he were to sleep as much as possible, there would be hours and hours to get through every day. He couldn't hang around the streets for more than a few of them. It was tiring and, in the end, depressing. To stay in shape, to keep his wits about him, he needed regular distractions, like this one, and he needed to make them last as long as he could.

Finally he wrote:

Tuesday, December 28—Departure from Juvisy by the window. Two women on the train. Rue Fromentin with Jeanne. She didn't laugh. I was careful only to stun her. Am sure to see her again.

Wednesday, December 29—Slept at faubourg Montmartre with a woman whose name I forgot to ask. Called me "sad." Bought toiletries. Wrote to Commissioner Lucas and played chess. In perfect form.

Which was enough. He knew it, because it brought everything to mind so clearly that he even remembered the suitcase—a tiny detail. He hadn't bought a suitcase so as not to become "the man with a suitcase." The most important thing was to avoid any obvious characteristics. And now, looking at himself in the mirror, he realized that one thing that was sure to enter into any description of him was his cigar. Those two young men, for instance—they wouldn't forget his having smoked one. Nor would the waiter in the restaurant where he'd written the letter. He looked around: out of some fifty customers only two were smoking cigars.

Jeanne Rozier knew about it. And Goin. And the hostess at Picratt's. The woman he'd left at noon had also noticed.

So if he didn't want to be identified as "the man with the cigar," he'd have to smoke something else—a pipe or cigarettes.

There was no other way—reluctant as he was to resign himself to the fact. His cigar was almost a part of him.

But once he'd arrived at his decision, it was effective immediately. After stubbing out the remnant of his cigar, he began to put tobacco into the ridiculous pipe he'd bought in Juvisy.

By now Commissioner Lucas must be conducting his investigation at the rue Fromentin. He'd question the concierge and, most likely, the two tenants Kees had run into in the lobby. He thought how funny it would be if he gave him a call: "Commissioner Lucas? Kees Popinga here. How about that little tip of mine? See what a good sport I am? I'm giving you the advantage."

It was too risky, though. The phone lines might be tapped—not that that was going to stop him from having his fun. There was a phone booth in a corner of the room. He bought some tokens and called up the three newspapers that had run the longest articles. At the editorial offices of the third, he even asked for the writer.

"Hello? Last night in Paris Kees Popinga attacked again. See for yourself at 13, rue Fromentin . . . Yes . . . What?"

At the other end of the line, a voice repeated: "Who is this? . . . Is that you, Marchandeau?"

They must think he was one of the paper's regular informants!

"No, not Marchandeau! Popinga! Good night, Monsieur Saladin! Try not to write any more nonsense. I'm not crazy, you know!"

He took his hat and overcoat and went downstairs. He'd decided to stay around the Bastille that night, so he headed off in that direction, always on foot.

It was his only option: not just changing restaurants and hotels, but changing the whole class of place he frequented. Twice he'd stayed at hotels of the same sort; now he'd bet anything that they'd be looking for him in similar places. Before the night was over, he bet, Commissioner Lucas would have checked out every single fleabag hotel in the whole of Montmartre.

Just like the two kids he'd played chess with—expecting him to make the same move twice!

He'd decided that at the Bastille he'd eat a prix fixe for some four or five francs. Then he'd find a ten-franc hotel.

He wasn't sure if he meant to sleep alone or if he'd pick up someone the way he already had twice.

He thought about it as he walked up the rue Saint-Antoine. He knew it could be a lot riskier than the suitcase or the cigar. He imagined the note in the police files: "Spending the night with hookers in hotels."

The police would be watching the places wherever there were girls in the streets.

He decided it wasn't safe.

And it wouldn't be safe to play chess at a different location every day either. "Spends afternoons playing chess in Paris cafés," his description would soon read.

At least that's what Kees would have put on a wanted poster, if he'd been in the commissioner's shoes, along with the fact that his pockets contained a razor, a shaving brush, shaving soap, and a toothbrush.

And suppose something of the sort appeared in all the Paris papers . . .

Walking in the crowd, past the lighted windows, he had to smile as he imagined the consequences.

In all the cafés where chess was played, the clientele would be glancing at one another suspiciously. During games the waiters might even rifle the pockets of overcoats—especially the gray ones—to make sure they didn't contain a razor or shaving brush.

As for the hookers, they'd see Popinga in every client. The police would be overwhelmed with a mass of tips!

"I shouldn't do it," he repeated.

Still, he was already tempted to become the character he'd sketched out. But he resisted the temptation. He forced himself to keep calm. He decided on some distraction. He'd see a movie after dinner.

He ate a five-franc prix fixe, but ended up spending eleven, since he couldn't turn down the extra portions. The waitresses were women in white aprons, and he wondered what they thought about him. To see what would happen, he gave a five-franc tip.

That would surprise her, wouldn't it? Wouldn't she take a closer look, connecting this man in a gray suit with a foreign accent to the sex fiend who was in all the papers?

Not at all! She stuffed the money in her apron pocket and went back to work. He might as well have left her two francs or a mere fifty centimes!

The movie theater was across the street: the Cinema Saint-Paul. He took a balcony seat because he didn't mind being seen. The usher was a girl in red, almost like the fellow at the Hotel Carlton in Amsterdam.

He figured he'd experiment with another, opposite, approach: this one he didn't tip at all. She just walked off grumbling. She was through with him.

So the day had come! They'd forgotten about him! He was surrounded by a conspiracy of silence!

Jeanne Rozier hadn't called the police. The papers had stopped reporting on the investigation. Goin's lips were sealed. Louis was in Marseille, and all the woman from this morning would remember was that he was another of those sad men she saw so often.

He'd never gone to the movies in Groningen: Mother considered them low-class. In any case they subscribed, in the winter, to a Thursday-night concert series. That was distraction enough.

There was something almost feverish in the air at the Cinema Saint-Paul. He'd never seen anything like it. There was a crowd of some two thousand people, all jammed together, eating oranges and sour drops.

Behind him the room was huge, and when he turned he saw hundreds of faces lit by the glow from the screen. It was a new experience.

Suppose somebody suddenly cried out, "That's him! The sex fiend from Amsterdam! The one who—"

But on all sides the balconies were filled with fat women in fur coats, young women with plump red hands, heavy-set men—a mix of the usual neighborhood types.

He had a dizzy spell at the intermission and didn't dare join the crowd that was streaming toward the bar and toilets. He watched the ads on the movie screen, and a furniture set for sale reminded him of the one they'd purchased in Groningen. Mother had sent away for catalogs from every shop in Holland.

What was Mother up to at this very moment? What was she thinking? She'd been the only one to mention an attack of amnesia, probably because the *Telegraaf* had printed a war novel in which a shell-shocked German soldier forgot everything, including his own name, and returned home ten years later to find that his wife had remarried and that his children no longer knew who he was.

And Julius de Coster? He'd said all sorts of things in the Little St. George, but drunk as he was, he knew better than to say where he was going. Popinga would have guessed London instead of Paris. De Coster knew London better. No doubt he had some cash hidden away there. He'd start a new business under an assumed name. He'd be making money again!

While the crowd returned to their seats, the lights dimmed and a purple light filled the screen. An orchestra played something slow and tender that brought tears to Popinga's eyes.

When the music ended, he clapped loudly along with the rest of the audience. He didn't care for the feature film, however, which was a story about a lawyer and his various professional secrets.

The fat woman next to him was wearing a mink coat—she was the best-dressed person in the balcony. She kept saying to her husband, "Why doesn't he tell the truth? He's a fool!"

Then it was time to go, a slow shuffle toward the cold, black tunnel of the street, where the stores were all closed, the cars driving away.

Popinga had spotted a hotel on the corner of the rue de Birague. From the looks of it, it would be cramped and extremely cheap.

It was the kind of place he was looking for: some fifty yards off he saw the silhouette of a woman lurking in the shadows.

Pick her up? Or not? Of course he'd already resolved . . .

But that wasn't important yet—it was still too early for the police to know.

The truth was he didn't like being alone at night, and especially not in the morning when he woke up. It reduced him to staring in the mirror and making different faces at himself: "If I had a mouth like this or a nose like that . . ."

Fine, then. One more time, that's it—if only to find out what kind of woman you found in a dark back street like this. He walked by, hands in his pockets, looking uninterested. Just as expected, she asked, "Want some company?"

He pretended to be reluctant, but then he turned. He saw a pale young face with a downcast look in the gaslight. The girl's threadbare coat was too light for the cold; her unbrushed hair hung down from a beret.

"She'll do," he made up his mind.

He followed her. He knew how these things worked by now. They passed a desk where a fat woman was playing patience.

"Room 7," she decided.

How about that? Room 7 again!

There was no bathroom—just a curtain in front of the porcelain sink. Popinga unpacked his soap, razor, and shaving brush without a glance at his companion.

"You're going to stay the whole night?"

"Of course."

"Okay."

She didn't seem happy about it, but too bad!

"You're not from around here?"

"Not at all."

"You're a foreigner?"

"What about you?"

"I'm from Brittany," she said, taking off her beret. "You'll be nice, won't you? You were at the movies, I saw you leave . . ."

She spoke just to say something, maybe to please him, and it did have the effect of making the place seem a little less empty. He washed carefully, checked the bed to see that it was at least somewhat clean, and lay down with a sigh of pleasure.

Another person he would have liked to get a glimpse of: Lucas's wife. What did *he* have to say for himself as he climbed into bed? Because at some point even he slept, just like everyone else.

"Do you want me to leave the light on?"

She was so thin that he preferred to look away.

8

On the difficulty of disposing of old newspapers and on the usefulness of a fountain pen and watch.

THAT MORNING there was almost nothing to write in the red notebook:

> Her name is Zulma. Gave her twenty francs and she was too scared to complain. As I was getting dressed she sighed and said, "I bet you like girls with a little more flesh on their bones. If you'd told me, I could have brought my friend."
>   "It doesn't matter."

He also made a note to buy a watch. When he was out, he could rely on the public clocks and the clocks in cafés. But it was inconvenient not knowing what time it was in the morning.

Only eight o'clock, and he was already out and about—fooled by the early-morning racket in the neighborhood.

Zulma left, her green coat hanging from her shoulders. Popinga approached a newsstand. His heart beat faster.

At last every one of the papers had something about him: two or three columns on all the front pages. He didn't see his picture, but then they'd already printed the only one they had. Instead there was Jeanne Rozier and her bedroom.

He had to restrain himself from buying all the papers all at once and running off to a café to read them.

It was hard to stay calm with so much space devoted to him alone, and no doubt there would be all sorts of different opinions expressed! People walked by. They picked up a paper before hurrying to the Métro.

He chose three of the dailies to begin with, the three biggest ones, and went to sit in a café on the place de la Bastille. He ordered a coffee and read and reread, now delighted, now furious, but always with the same feverish intensity. No one guessed the storms that were raging within him.

He wanted to hold on to the articles—that he knew. But how, practically speaking, was he going to handle it? He couldn't walk around with a dozen of them stuffed into his pockets.

He considered the question. Eventually, he went downstairs to the bathroom and cut out all the articles about him with his penknife. All that was left to do was to get rid of the remnants. He figured the best thing would be to flush them down the toilet. It cost him a good half hour's work, though, since the wad of paper wouldn't flush. He had to pull the chain again and again and wait for the tank to refill. Back upstairs, everybody must have assumed he'd been sick.

He'd have to change tactics. Over the course of the day he bought something like twenty papers, but never more than three at time, lest he attract attention.

The first set of three he read in a restaurant at the intersection of the boulevard Henri-IV and the Seine. He threw the cut-up pages into the river.

The next batch took him to a café on the quai d'Austerlitz. Moving downriver, he finally reached the quai de Bercy.

He couldn't find a place he liked in the neighborhood, so in the afternoon he headed back to the streets around the Gare de Lyon. He found a restaurant that appealed to him with a secluded corner behind the stove. He'd bought a fountain pen, having left his own in Groningen. At two in the afternoon, he set to work.

Eighty-five francs for the watch and thirty-two for the pen: he had serious work ahead, so he'd been willing to spend the money. It was no use writing with the kind of pen they lend to customers in cafés—he knew that now.

All he needed was some paper. Then he set to work, writing in a small, neat hand. He knew he'd be at it for a long time, and he didn't want his wrist to get tired.

"To the Editor," he wrote. The letter was addressed to the largest newspaper in Paris. They'd printed nearly three whole columns about him and even sent a reporter to Holland for several days. Kees had singled it out both because of the size of its circulation and because it was the only paper which had something smart to say: "Pamela's murderer is playing a game of cat and mouse with the police. He has recently informed them of a new crime he has committed."

He had lots of time. He would choose his words carefully. The stove snored like the stove in Groningen. There were customers at all the tables, quietly waiting for their trains.

To the Editor:

First of all, I hope you'll make allowances for my French, because these last few years in Holland I haven't had much opportunity to practice.

Think of it, people who don't know you at all are writing that you're like this or like that in all the papers, when in fact none of it's true, you're completely different. I'm sure you yourself wouldn't be too happy about that and would want to tell the truth.

Your reporter went to Groningen and interviewed various people, but not one of them knows a thing. That, or they meant to tell lies or they simply couldn't help themselves.

I would like to set the record straight. I'll begin at the beginning, because I hope you'll print this document which actually does tell the truth and will show how someone may become the victim of the opinions of others.

Your article talks, among other things, about my family. It accepts the testimony of my wife. She told your reporter: "I can't understand what happened; there was no way anyone could have foreseen anything. Kees came from a good family; he had a good education. When he married me, he was a thoughtful and mature young man whose only ambition was to start a family of his own. He has been a good husband and father for sixteen years. His health was excellent, but last month, on an icy night, he slipped and hit his head—I should mention that. Maybe there was some sort of injury to his brain, something that caused a fit of amnesia? Certainly he can't have been in his right mind when he did what he did. He shouldn't be held responsible."

———

Kees ordered another coffee. He almost asked for a cigar, but he remembered his decision. He sighed with dismay as he filled his pipe before rereading the previous lines. He began to make his case.

This is what I have to say on this subject:

1. I am not from a good family. But you can understand why my wife, whose father was a mayor, would say that to the press. My mother was a midwife. My father was an architect. But it was my mother who supported us. My father was friendly and outgoing and he liked to spend time drinking with his clients. Afterward he neglected to bill them, or neglected to do the work, so his troubles were endless.

He was never discouraged, however. With a groan he would say he was just too nice a guy.

But that's not how my mother saw it. I don't remember a day passing without a scene at the house. When my father drank, the quarrels got really violent. My mother would scream at me and my sister, "Look at him! Don't be like him! He's going to drive me to my grave!"

2. So you see my wife wasn't telling the truth. And not about my education, either. I did study for the Merchant Marine, but I never had any money and so it was impossible for me to go out and have fun with friends. It made me resentful and double-dealing.

Which is to say that, though we were very poor at home, we hid it from everybody else. For example, even on days when there was nothing to eat for dinner except some bread, my mother put two or three pots on the stove in case someone happened to drop in. That way she could pretend she was preparing a magnificent meal.

I met my wife when I was almost through with my studies. Now, because it's the done thing, she'd like to believe we were in love with each other.

But it isn't true. My wife lived in a little village where her father was the mayor. What she wanted was to live in a real town like Groningen.

I was flattered to marry the daughter of a man who was so rich and respectable—a girl who'd gone to boarding school till she was eighteen.

Otherwise I would have gone to sea. But she said, "I'll never marry a sailor. They drink too much. They run around with women."

———

He knew the article almost by heart, but he took it out of his pocket and reread it.

3. According to Mrs. Popinga, it seems that for sixteen years I was a good husband and father. That's no more accurate than the rest. Maybe I never cheated on my wife, but you can't do that in Groningen without everyone finding out, and Mrs. Popinga would have made my life impossible.

She wouldn't have wept, the way my mother did. She would have done what she did when I bought something on impulse that she didn't approve of or when I smoked too many cigars. She'd say, "How nice." Then she wouldn't speak to me for two or three days running, going about the house as if she were the unhappiest woman in the world. If the children noticed, she'd reply with a moan, "Your father's so cruel. He doesn't understand!" I'd be surrounded by reproaches and tears.

Because I'm a good-natured man, I preferred to avoid any scenes. So for sixteen years the deal was that I got one night off a week for chess or the occasional game of billiards.

At my mother's, I had visions of riches, the way everybody does. I wanted money so I could have fun in town with my friends. And I had visions of nice clothes—not my father's hand-me-downs.

At my house—my wife's house, that is—I spent sixteen years full of envy for men who go out at night without having to say where—the ones you see with pretty girls hanging from their arms, the men on the trains that are going far away.

As to being a good father—I don't believe I was. I never detested my children. The day they were born I said they were beautiful in order to make my wife happy, but in fact I thought they were hideous and I haven't really changed my mind since.

People claim my daughter's smart because she never says a word, but I know that's only because she has nothing to say. And she's a snob too, putting on airs when she shows her friends the nice little house she lives in. Once I happened to overhear the following conversation:

"What does your father do?"

"He's the head man at the de Coster company."

Which was a lie. Do you see? As for the boy, he has none of the faults you'd expect at his age, which makes me think that he's sure to amount to nothing.

If people say I'm a good father because I found time to play games with my children, they're wrong. We play games in the evening because I was bored. I was always bored. I built a big house not because I wanted one, but because when I was young I envied my friends who lived in big houses.

I bought the same stove as I had seen in the house of my richest friend. The same desk as . . .

But this isn't getting us anywhere. I wasn't a child from a good family and I didn't have a good education and I wasn't a good husband or a good father, and if my wife says I was, it's to persuade herself that she has been a good wife and mother and all the rest.

———

It was only three in the afternoon. He had time to think about things. He stared off into the increasingly murky atmosphere of the café. Outside it was getting dark.

I also read in your article that Basinger, my accountant at de Coster, said: "Mr. Popinga was so attached to the company that he almost considered it his personal property. The news of its failure must have come as a terrible shock. It may have unhinged his mind."

I must tell you, my dear sir, such things are painful to read. What if somebody told you that for the rest of your life you'd be eating nothing but black bread and sausage? Wouldn't you try to make yourself believe that black bread and sausage are the best things in the world?

For sixteen years I persuaded myself that the de Coster company was the most stable and solid in Holland.

Then, one night, at the Little St. George (you won't understand, but it doesn't matter), I learned that Julius de Coster was a scoundrel and a lot of other hard truths.

Not "scoundrel." That's the wrong word. All in all, and without shouting it from the rooftops, Julius de Coster did everything I'd always wanted to do. He had a mistress, Pamela, who . . .

But I'll get to that. Just realize that for the first time in my life I looked at myself in the mirror and I asked, "Why in the world do I want to go on living like this?"

Yes, why? Maybe you'll ask yourself the same question. Maybe a lot of your readers will ask it, too. Why? What's the reason? There wasn't any! I took a long, hard look at some things we never look at except from one lousy point of view, and that's what I discovered.

All things considered, it was out of sheer habit that I stayed in my job, or stayed married, or was a father to my children. All of it—sheer habit. And who'd decided that things would be like that and not otherwise? I don't know!

And what if I wanted to be something else?

Once you've made up your mind on that point, once you've decided to make a change, you can't imagine how straightforward everything else is. You no longer have to worry about what so-and-so thinks, about what you can or can't do, about whether this is the right way to do something or not.

Back home, for example, even when I was going no farther than the next town, my bags had to be packed, a call was made to reserve a room . . .

And me? I went to the train station without the slightest worry and bought a ticket to Amsterdam, good for forever!

And because Julius de Coster had told me about Pamela, and because for two years I'd wanted her more than any other woman in the world, I went to see her.

It's all so simple, isn't it? She asked me what I wanted, and I told her straight out, precisely the way I'm writing to you, but instead of finding it the most natural thing in the world, she burst out into idiotic and insulting laughter.

What difference did it make to her? That's what I want to know. Didn't she do it for a living, anyway? As for me, my mind was made up: I meant to have her. No matter what. The next day I found out that I tugged a little too hard on the towel. Maybe Pamela had a weak heart.

Has anyone investigated that? Somebody should, because it's pretty surprising how easily she gave up the ghost.

So here too your reporter got it all wrong. What does he say? That I fled Groningen like a madman! That other passengers could tell I was demented! That on the boat the steward clearly noticed something wrong!

But what nobody understands is that it was "before" when something was wrong. "Before," if I wanted a drink, I was afraid to say as much, afraid to go into a bar. If I got hungry at somebody's house and they offered me something to eat, I'd murmur politely, "Thank you, no."

On a train, I thought I had to pretend to read or stare at the countryside. I kept my gloves on, even when they were too tight. That was the proper thing to do.

Your reporter goes on: "The criminal then made a crucial mistake that would lead to others: in his frenzy, he left his briefcase behind in the victim's room."

It's not true! I didn't make a mistake! I wasn't in a frenzy! I'd brought the briefcase along out of habit and I didn't need it anymore. Might as well leave it there as anywhere else! And I would have written to the police anyway once I found out Pamela was dead—to let them know who was to blame.

And the proof is that only yesterday I express-mailed a message to Commissioner Lucas telling him I had attacked someone else—Jeanne Rozier.

Your headline was obviously intended to flatter me. Saying that I was playing cat and mouse with the French police! But that's not it, either. I'm not playing games with anyone, and I don't want to. And I'm not a sex fiend or evil. That's not why I assaulted Jeanne Rozier.

It's hard to explain what happened. It's a little bit like the whole story with Pamela. For two days in a row I was free to do whatever I wanted with Jeanne Rozier. I just wasn't tempted.

Then, all at once, I thought about it and I realized I had to have her. So I went and told her. And for no good reason she refused.

Why? And why shouldn't I have just gone ahead and used force? So I did, but I was careful, because she's a sweet woman really. I didn't want anything bad to happen. Or to Pamela! That was an accident. It was my first time!

So do you start to see why yesterday's articles are so annoying? I'm not going to write to every newspaper. That's too much work. But this is something I have to clear up.

I'm not crazy. I'm not a sex fiend. I just decided, at the age of forty, to live as I please, without bothering about the law or convention. I'd learned late in life that no one else does anyway and all that time I'd simply had the wool pulled over my eyes.

I don't know what I'll do next, or if there will be anything else to keep the police busy. Depends on how I feel.

I'm a peaceful man, no matter what everyone must think. Tomorrow I may meet a woman who's worth the trouble. If I do, I'll marry her and never be heard from again.

On the other hand, if you push me too hard and I feel like a fight to the finish, I don't think there's anything that could stop me.

For forty years I've been bored. For forty years, I looked at life like a poor boy with his nose glued to the pastry-shop window, watching the other people eat cake.

Now I know that the cake belongs to the people who are willing to take it.

Go on printing that I'm a nut if you want to. That just

proves you're crazy, the way I was before the Little St. George.

In exchange for printing this letter, I relinquish any right of response. No doubt some will smile to hear that. But only idiots. Because who but a man who has actually put his life on the line has the right to demand a correction for the untruths that are being published about him?

As I wait to read this in your pages, I am your devoted (not that it's true, but that's the formula),

Kees Popinga

His wrist ached, but he hadn't had such a good time in ages. He could hardly bring himself to stop writing. The gaslights had come on. Across the way the clock at the train station read 4:30 PM. Nothing could be more normal—a customer passing the hours by catching up with his correspondence—that's what the waiter would think.

"To the Editor."

This time he was writing to a paper that had printed "THE DUTCH NUT CASE" in bold letters. He replied,

Your reporter must have a high opinion of himself. Probably he composes advertising slogans more often than he writes real journalism.

First, I don't see what being Dutch has to do with any of this. I've read a lot more horrifying news stories in which the villain is a good Frenchman.

Second, it's easy to call someone you don't understand crazy.

If this is how you seek to keep your readers informed,
I am prevented from closing,

> With every respect,
> Kees Popinga

Two down!

For a moment he thought about paying a repeat visit to the boulevard Saint-Michel and playing a game of chess. Then again, yesterday he'd decided never to go back to the same place twice; he wanted to stick to his resolution. Plus there was a newsboy going from table to table, hawking the evening papers. Kees bought them and started to read.

It can only be a matter of days until the arrest of Popinga, the Amsterdam sex fiend. Police Commissioner Lucas is tireless and the net he has cast grows ever tighter. Escape is impossible.

We offer no apologies for saying no more. It will be clear that to reveal any of the measures currently being taken would only play into the criminal's hands.

Jeanne Rozier, the Dutchman's latest victim, is said to be in satisfactory condition. Her assailant is reported to have insufficient funds to remain at large for much longer.

Let it also be said that he has a number of distinctive habits that make him easy to recognize. Beyond that, of course, we cannot elaborate.

Only one thing is to be feared: if cornered, Popinga may strike again. Precautions have been taken against this possibility.

The commissioner displayed his usual calm when he addressed the press recently, explaining that there are several English and German precedents for this case, fortunately rare in the annals of crime.

Sex fiends are often victims of abuse themselves. They lack a sense of conscience, but can be highly intelligent. Their very self-confidence may, however, lead them to commit a fatal mistake.

For this reason, arrest is at most a question of days, perhaps even hours. Various leads have already been followed up. This morning a female passenger at the Gare de l'Est reported a suspicious person answering to Popinga's description. An arrest was made, but authorities identified the suspect as a respectable businessman from the Strasbourg area.

A small complication for investigators is Kees Popinga's fluent command of four languages, making it possible for him to pass as English, Dutch, or German.

On questioning, Jeanne Rozier at first refused to divulge any information. The detailed description that she did finally provide is likely to prove invaluable to the police.

The public may rest assured: Kees Popinga will not escape.

———

Funny—if anything, the article made him optimistic. He went downstairs to the bathroom to look at himself in the mirror.

He hadn't lost weight. He was in top-notch shape. For a moment he thought about dyeing his hair or letting his beard grow. Except they were less likely to be looking for him as he was, he told himself, than under some sort of disguise.

The same went for his gray suit. It couldn't be more ordinary.

"The one thing is, it would be better to have a blue overcoat," he decided.

So he paid the check, mailed off his letters at the train

station, and headed to an off-the-rack place he'd seen that morning near the Bastille.

"I'm looking for a blue overcoat—navy blue."

As he spoke to the clerk on the second floor of the department store, he became aware of a new danger, another of his little tics: he'd developed the habit of looking at people ironically—as if to say, "So, what do you think? You haven't seen the newspapers? Don't you realize you're waiting on the notorious Popinga, the Dutch Nut Case?"

He tried on several overcoats—all of them too small or too tight. At last he found one that seemed more or less right, even if the quality was poor.

"I'll take this," he announced.

"Where would you like the other sent?"

"Just wrap it up, please. I'll take it with me."

Little things like that were a risk. Like walking around in the streets wearing a new overcoat with a package under his arm! Luckily it was dark and the Seine was nearby. He'd get rid of his awkward burden there.

The journalists said ridiculous things about him, but they helped him out too. They gave him clues to what Commissioner Lucas might be thinking.

Unless . . . well, obviously, unless the commissioner was dictating the stories in order to trip him up.

The whole situation was just too weird. He didn't know the commissioner, and the commissioner didn't know him. They'd never even laid eyes on each other. They were like two players, two chess players, going head to head without being able to see the other's pieces.

What were the measures the papers were talking about? Why did they seem to believe he'd strike again?

They were trying to provoke him, that was it!

For Christ's sake! They seemed to think the slightest suggestion would set him off! They figured that even if he wasn't stark raving mad, he was troubled! They were needling him, goading him on to commit a new crime in the hope that he'd make a mistake.

What kind of description could Jeanne Rozier have given them? Everybody already knew he wore gray. That he smoked cigars? That he had no more than three thousand francs in his pocket? That he hadn't shaved?

No, he wasn't going to worry about it. But not to know what was on the commissioner's mind—that was a bit of a worry. What instructions had he given his men? Where were they looking? And how?

Maybe Lucas thought Popinga would want to see the car thieves arrested, that he'd come prowling around the garage in Juvisy.

Never!

Or that he'd go on hanging around Montmartre?

Not likely!

So when, how, did he think he was going to catch him?

Was he hoping that Kees would try to escape? Would he have the train stations watched?

Popinga started glancing over his back from time to time—he couldn't help it. On top of that, he kept stopping in front of shop windows to make sure no one was following him. Standing in front of the map by an entrance to the Métro, he asked himself which part of town he'd choose that night. Yes, which one?

The cops would be making the rounds in at least one neighborhood that night; maybe two or three. They'd visit every flophouse, demand papers from everyone they found.

But which one would Lucas pick? And why should Kees go to bed at all, when he wasn't even tired? The day before, on one of the boulevards, he'd seen a theater that screened movies continuously until six in the morning. Would Lucas think of looking in a place like that?

In any case, what he had to do, no matter what, was to stop giving that ironic look to people, especially women—as if he was saying, "Don't you recognize me? Aren't you scared?"

Because he'd begun to seek out such situations. The proof of this was that without even realizing it, he'd once again settled on a restaurant where the staff was entirely female.

"Be careful how you look at people"—he stopped under a streetlamp to jot that down.

One sentence in that last article had really gotten to him. The writer insisted that most likely he'd end up giving himself away.

How had they guessed? Guessed that what he couldn't stand was the feeling of being all alone in a crowd, that in such situations he was seized by a kind of vertigo, that sometimes—especially when he ran into someone in a dark deserted street—he wanted to come right out with it and demand: "Don't you know who I am?"

But he'd been warned and now he was out of danger. He got back into the habit of looking at people unselfconsciously, like some nobody, instead of the man all the newspapers were talking about.

What in fact had gone through Julius de Coster's mind when he found out? Because he had to know by now. The English and German papers were all talking about it, too.

He, at least, would have to admit he'd been all wrong about his employee. At the Little Saint-George, he'd told his secrets as if to an idiot, someone incapable of understanding. He must be pretty embarrassed now.

Because the boss had been shown up by his employee. Popinga had crushed Julius! There were no two ways about it. Somewhere—London, Hamburg, Berlin—Julius was trying to set up some sort of respectable, serious business. And in the meantime Popinga, with brutal frankness, was letting the whole world know just what he thought.

One of these days, simply to check out de Coster's reaction, he'd go ahead and place that ad in the *Morning Post*, as they'd arranged. But how would he hear back?

Popinga kept walking. It had become the better part of his life—this wandering the streets in the light of the shop windows as the crowd brushed past indifferently. His hands felt around mechanically for the toothbrush, shaving brush, and safety razor in his overcoat pockets.

Now he had the answer! He knew he could always count on himself to find the answer, just as in chess. All he'd have to do was to stay two times at the same hotel and write himself two letters under an assumed name. Then he'd have two envelopes addressed to him, which was all he'd need later as proof of identity to pick up mail from general delivery.

Why not begin that very night? Once more, he slipped into a café. He didn't like the real Parisian cafés: the tables were too small, the drinkers jammed up against one another. He was used to places in Holland, where there was no risk of touching a neighbor's elbow.

"Give me a phone book."

He opened it at random to the rue Brey. He didn't know the street. He picked out the name of a hotel, the Beauséjour.

Then he wrote a letter to himself. That is, he slipped a sheet of paper into an envelope on which he wrote "Mr. Smitson, Hôtel Beauséjour, 14A, rue Brey."

Why not save time and write both letters at once? He disguised his handwriting. Now he had the second envelope.

He'd send it express.

And why not make the most of it and demand that de Coster pay him off? He must be frightened to death that Kees would blow his cover.

He wrote the ad: "Kees to Julius. Send five thousand c/o Smitson, General Delivery, Post Office 42, Paris."

These chores kept him busy until eleven at night. He didn't hurry; he took his time. He took pleasure in his elegant handwriting, fine and legible.

"Waiter! Some stamps, please!"

Then he went down to the phone booth and requested the Beauséjour. He spoke in English at first before switching to French with a strong cross-Channel accent.

"Hello! Smitson here. I'll be arriving at your hotel tomorrow morning. I'm expecting some mail. Can you hold it for me?"

"Certainly, sir."

Would the commissioner be devastated? Could he ever have imagined Popinga's utter aplomb?

"Would you like a room with a bath?"

"Of course."

And yet even so he'd almost been shaken—solely because it had been a woman's voice on the other end of the line. But never mind. That was what he had to avoid at any cost. It was clear from the evening papers that they were expecting him to strike again, providing new information to the police.

"But I won't do it!" he decided. "And the proof is I'm going to make it a quiet night at the movies. Tomorrow, at six in the morning, I'll arrive at the Beauséjour as if I'd just arrived on the train."

He'd thought of everything! In another café he asked for the train schedule, which was all the more evidence of his foresight; there was a train in from Strasbourg at 5:32.

"So I'm due to arrive from Strasbourg!"

That was it—the job was done and he could go to the movies. It was reassuring that the ushers weren't working girls, but strapping youths in uniform.

What would Commissioner Lucas do? And Louis, who by now must be back from Marseille? And Goin? And Rose, who, for no particular reason, he loathed?

9

The girl in blue satin and the young man with a broken nose.

WHAT DID it matter to the newspapers if they printed a few words more or less? Usually they laid it on with a trowel, letting readers in on what the police were thinking about one thing or another, or that they'd set a certain kind of trap, publishing a group portrait of the team charged with tracking down the criminal.

But none of the papers, Popinga had noted, not one, had printed a picture of Commissioner Lucas. Obviously, it didn't make that much difference. The commissioner wasn't going to run around town in person, like a bloodhound, hot on Kees's trail. Still, Kees would have liked to know what his adversary looked like. It would have helped him to form an opinion.

It wasn't the silence of the newspapers that troubled him so much as the thought that they were under orders. For example, the paper that had published Popinga's long letter had introduced it with the following story:

Police Commissioner Lucas read the letter through with a smile and handed it back with a shrug.

"What do you make of it?" he was asked.

"He's done for," is all the commissioner replied.

Which meant nothing, Popinga realized, but it was no help at all either. What he would have liked to know, among other things, was whether the girl whose name he hadn't learned, the one he'd taken up to the room in Montmartre and who'd bought him the razor—whether she'd later recognized him and made a statement to the police.

That was important. Because if it got around that he carried a razor and shaving brush in his pockets he'd soon be found out, unless he made up his mind to spend all his nights alone.

And sleeping alone was no fun. He'd done it at the Hotel Beauséjour on the rue Brey, where he'd picked up the two letters that would allow him to check in at general delivery as Smitson.

The day after that he had slept by himself again at a hotel in the Vaugirard, but in the middle of the night he'd almost left to search someone out. Strange—when there was a woman with him, he fell asleep right away and slept straight through until morning. But when he was on his own, his thoughts got going, slowly at first, like a vehicle approaching the top of a hill, but then they went faster and faster, thoughts of all sorts of things, unpleasant things, all rushing together until at last he had to sit up in bed and turn on the light.

If he'd told someone, maybe they'd say he was feeling remorse. It wasn't true, though. What proved it was that his thoughts kept going back to Jeanne Rozier, who he'd barely touched and who would never have willingly turned him in, while he gave no thought at all to Pamela, who was dead. Rose, too, he could see in his mind's eye: she'd been mean to him, though he hadn't done anything to her. Why, with so many phantoms around, had she turned into his wicked stepmother? And why did he go on dreaming that Jeanne Rozier was staring at him with her green eyes, with a look that was both tender and ironic, before kissing his eyelashes and laying a cool hand on his?

Was it better to toss and turn all night long or to run the risk that some streetwalker would identify him? None of the reporters, not one, was going to be so kind, or stupid, as to write: "The police are in possession of the following information... The following places will be under observation..."

He'd written his letters, including the one he'd sent off to Commissioner Lucas, in different cafés. So would they start watching all the cafés? Even if they didn't, the situation was dangerous: it's a waiter's business to keep an eye on people. Plus they read the papers, and they have all the time in the world to scrutinize their customers.

Why didn't the papers come right out: "This very day, five strangers who requested writing materials from cafés downtown were turned over to the police and brought in for identification."

That was why Popinga had to be ever more careful. And tonight he felt especially concerned.

True, the real problem was that it was New Year's eve. In most of the cafés, you couldn't even find a seat. They were busy preparing for tonight's dinner. Waiters stood on the tables to hang sprigs of mistletoe and paper streamers from the ceiling.

Popinga remembered Christmas Eve, a week ago. He'd been at the café on the rue de Douai, and Jeanne Rozier had stopped in twice to see him. She'd taken the trouble, even though she was with Louis and his friends. Then there'd been the strange trip in a stolen car, the arrival at Juvisy, snow on the train yard and all those trains, the wheezing of the locomotives, the dull thud of the bumpers as they shunted the cars...

He walked... He'd walked a lot over the last two days. He did it to show his disdain for the waiters in the cafés, and when he stopped it was in one of those little bistros that are in every neighborhood—the ones that are empty for the most part so you have to wonder how they ever make any money.

He was afraid to sleep. Would Commissioner Lucas be out celebrating? Where would he go if he did go out on New Year's Eve?

He was tired. But that would be over with the holidays, when Paris would no longer be gripped by the exhausting compulsion to have fun, whatever the cost.

He felt scarily tempted to revisit the flower vendor on the rue Douai, and instead he decided to spend the night in a neighborhood on the other side of town. It was the Gobelins, which seemed to him one of the saddest parts of Paris, with wide streets that weren't old but were already run-down, houses that were as drearily indistinguishable as barracks, cafés crowded with people who were neither rich nor poor.

And he ended up in a place of that very kind, where a sandwich board advertised a holiday meal for forty francs—champagne included.

"You're alone?" The waiter was astonished.

Not only was he alone, he was one of the first customers to arrive. He had time to observe all the little preparations, to see the members of the band come in, one after the other. They all chatted away as they tuned their instruments, and the waiters went around putting a sprig of mistletoe at every table setting and folding the napkins into fans, as if for a small-town wedding.

Then it was time for the customers to appear, and it seemed ever more like a wedding. So much so that, eventually, Popinga had to ask himself if it wouldn't be more prudent for him to leave.

Because everyone knew everybody, and there was a lot of to-ing and fro-ing among tables, so it was more or less a big party. It was all families—the kind that had been in the balcony of the Cinema Saint-Paul, the small shopkeepers of the neighborhood, scrubbed clean of course, drenched in cologne, and wearing their Sunday best, with all the women showing off their new dresses.

The room had been empty when Popinga came in, but it only took fifteen minutes for it to hum with conversation, laughter, music, the clinking of knives, forks, and glasses.

Everyone was in high spirits, too. They'd come to have fun, and from the word go they were pulling out all the stops—especially the women who were past their prime or had some flesh on their bones.

Kees took his meal along with the others, without giving it much thought. God knows why, but the atmosphere brought to mind the story of the powdered sugar in the oxtail soup, when his friend had received his professorship. Why was it that the papers seemed to be waiting for him to do something like attack Pamela again?

He was in a corner. Not far away, there was a big imposing character with a watch fob and what appeared to be a waxed mustache. He was wearing a dinner jacket that was a little too tight and presiding over a long table around which sat a number of families who were obviously well acquainted. From their conversation, Kees guessed that he must be some sort of local official.

His wife, stuffed into a black silk evening dress, was no less remarkable. On the front of her dress, as in a store window, there was a massive display of diamonds, perhaps real, perhaps fake.

Finally, there was the daughter, just to the left of the father. She resembled both parents without being ugly, and though eventually, no doubt, she'd come to look like her mother, for now she was still fresh, weirdly pink in her blue satin dress. She wasn't what you'd call fat yet, but she was plump, the bodice of her dress so tight that at moments it seemed she could hardly breathe.

What difference did it make to Popinga? He ate. He lent half an ear to the music. Between courses, the couples got up to dance, but he didn't even think of joining in as they swirled around the tables.

And yet, stupidly enough, that was exactly what happened. He was looking off in the direction of the young woman while thinking of something else when they struck up a new waltz. She must have taken his glance for an invitation. She smiled and made a gesture, as if to say, "Do you want to?"

She rose, smoothed the wrinkles from her dress, and came over to Popinga, who found himself in the midst of the couples. His partner had sweaty palms and she gave off a faint smell that wasn't at all disagreeable. She leaned on him with her full weight as she danced, crushing her bosom against him, while the parents looked on with approval.

Popinga, in fact, still felt somewhat out of it. He caught a glimpse of himself in the mirror, and he wondered if it was really his reflection. There was a wry smile on his lips. Big girl that she was, what would she have said if she'd known? . . .

Suddenly the band stopped dead. There was a hideous beating of the drums, and everyone shouted and laughed and kissed. Kees saw her soft face rising up to his. She kissed him on the cheeks.

Midnight! The people were milling around and laughing together, some making threats, others making out. Popinga was standing there, pretty much at a loss. The girl kissed him, then her father did, followed by another woman from the table who must have been the owner of a vegetable stand.

Streamers erupted on all sides—little balls of colored cotton that the waiters had hastily passed around. The band struck up again. Without meaning to, Popinga again found himself dancing with the girl in blue.

"Don't look to your left," she whispered in his ear.

And as the dance started up again, wilder than ever, she confided, "I don't know what he'll to do. Wait! Steer me over to the right side of the room. I'm totally terrified he's going to make a scene!"

"Who?"

"Don't look, or he'll know we're talking about him! You'll see him in a minute. He's young and he's wearing a dinner jacket. He's by himself. He's got dark skin and a scar on one side of his face. We were almost engaged, but then I broke it off because I found out about some things..."

All the champagne she'd drunk must have been making her talkative. True, the mood was one that encouraged making confidences, letting go, friendliness. They'd all kissed each other, hadn't they? And so it went, with people chasing into every corner of the room to find people they'd forgotten, women being pushed under bunches of mistletoe where a sudden kiss was sure to make them cry out in delight.

"I'm telling you because I think it's better that you know what you're getting into."

"Yes," he said noncommittally.

"Maybe it would be best if you didn't ask me to dance again. From what I know, he's capable of anything. And he's already warned me that he'll make sure I'm never engaged to another man."

Luckily the dance was over, and the girl went back to her place. The mother smiled discreetly at Popinga, as if he'd done a favor for the whole family.

Sitting in the corner, Kees looked around for the young man he'd been told about. He spotted him at once—the only person who fit the description. He did have a scar on one cheek. It made his face look even more crooked, especially since his nose was all bent out of shape.

He was furious—you could tell at a glance. He was pale and

his lips were trembling. His terrible eyes were fixed on the young girl in blue.

How come the whole thing looked like an amateur painting to Popinga, the colors garish, the figures fussed to death? There was an unexpected lull in the action, then the five members of the band filled the room with a sound like thunder. Everybody burst out laughing, going into hysterics over nothing—a streamer, a colored cotton ball hitting a man on the neck or nose. Everybody was happy, almost divinely happy, everybody except the young man with the broken nose, who seemed to be playing the bad guy in a provincial drama.

So Popinga's mistake was not to have drunk champagne with everyone else. If he had, he probably would have been left as utterly relaxed and expansive as the rest. He might have actually enjoyed seeing the New Year in with these crude displays of family feeling.

Every once in a while, the girl gave him a complicit glance. "Quite right!" she appeared to imply. "It's much better that you haven't asked me to dance. You can see for yourself how dangerous he is!"

What did the young man do? Was he a bank employee? He was fashionable, though—more like a salesman in a department store. In any case, a romantic fellow. All on his own he was living through a whole novel, a tragedy, with the blond daughter of the member of the local council as his chosen one.

The father danced with the mother, then with his daughter, then in succession with all the ladies at the table. He cavorted and joked, hamming it up, putting on a cardboard fireman's helmet and playing the chief.

There had been party favors all around. Popinga had received a white naval officer's cap. He was careful not to put it on.

The girl's mother turned to him repeatedly, always with the same insinuating smile: "Aren't you going to dance again?"

She was sure to have described him to her husband as "quite respectable-looking."

Meanwhile, there was somebody new dancing with the blue satin dress—a young man who'd popped out of some corner when Popinga wasn't paying attention. And suddenly Kees knew that the danger was very real. The fellow with the broken nose was looking on with a genuine tragic intensity.

The dance went on, and again and again it seemed like he was about to leap up. Popinga didn't like the way he kept his right hand in his pocket.

"Waiter!" he called out.

"Yes, sir, yes..."

He had a bad feeling about it. Something was about to happen, he was sure, and he wanted to get away as soon as possible. The others were all busy having fun. They didn't have any suspicion. But as far as he was concerned, the young man with the broken nose might as well have already gone ahead and caused a scene.

"Hey! Waiter?"

"Yes, sir. Surely you're not going already? It's not even one."

"What do I owe you?"

"Well, it's up to you... Let's see, now. Forty-eight and seven ...fifty-five francs."

Popinga was about to panic. Even a few seconds of delay was a tremendous risk; he could hardly stand to wait for his coat to come from the coat check. All the time, he kept an eye on the "bad guy." He was on his feet now, while the girl in blue went on dancing, and every time she danced around she flashed that same vague smile in Kees's face.

"Thanks."

He was in such a hurry to stand up that he nearly knocked the table over.

The mother looked at him reproachfully. Already going, it implied, and you didn't even ask me for a dance.

He reached the vestibule, hat still in hand. He was through the first door...

The shot rang out all too clearly over the noise of the band. A stupefied silence followed. Kees almost turned back. But he knew he had to resist that temptation no matter what. He was in danger. There was barely time for him to escape from this utterly commonplace café which had just been the site of an act of passion.

He turned left, then right. He took streets he'd never taken, walking fast, wondering if the girl in blue satin was dead and how she looked—a fat doll stretched out on the floor among the streamers and balls of cotton.

He'd already come a long way when he saw a police car racing in the direction of the Gobelins. Another fifteen minutes went by before he stopped again, surprised to see the boulevard Saint-Michel and, off to the left, the café where he'd played chess with the Japanese fellow.

It was only then that the fear hit him. He realized what a close call it had been. He wiped the sweat from his face. He could feel his knees trembling.

How dumb could it get? Here he was engaged in what could only be called a battle of wits with Commissioner Lucas and the whole world, including the press, and he was going to be caught because a jealous young man had fired off a shot?

From now on, he had to keep clear of crowds. Something was always happening in such situations, some drama, some accident, and the next thing you knew they asked for your papers.

He shouldn't be hanging around the boulevard Saint-Michel, either. Rightly or wrongly, he figured that that was one of the places they'd be out looking for him. Montmartre too. And Montparnasse. Better to go back to a part of town like the Gobelins. Find a quiet hotel, get some sleep...

Plus there was work to do, right? He hadn't written anything in his notebook since yesterday. Not, of course, that there was much to write—apart from the pistol shot . . .

But he'd reached another decision. The notebook wasn't enough. Something could happen to him and then no one would understand. So he'd made himself a promise. When he found the time, he was going to write his memoirs—the real story.

He'd gotten the idea from a newspaper that had published his letter. The headline they'd come up with had been A KILLER'S STRANGE CONFESSION.

Then, under the text of his letter, they'd run the following article:

> Readers will see that we have presented them a document of the highest human interest. It is rare to find such a specimen even in the archives of the police.
>
> How sincere is Kees Popinga? Is he playing a part? If he is, does he know it? Is he or isn't he insane? We can hardly presume to judge.
>
> Which is why we have submitted this letter for examination to two of our most celebrated psychiatrists. Tomorrow we expect to print their opinions in our columns. In doing so we are convinced that we will be providing a signal service to the police.

He'd reread the letter they referred to and hadn't been pleased. Printed in the newspaper his words and sentences didn't have the same ring as on the café stationery. Many things were badly explained. Others weren't explained at all. It was to the point where he almost wrote the two psychiatrists asking them to hold off before they rendered their opinions!

On the basis of what he'd said about his father, for example, people might think this was a case of hereditary alcoholism. In fact, however, his father hadn't begun to drink excessively until several years after Kees was born.

And he hadn't done a good job explaining that the reason why he'd always been such a loner, since he was a schoolboy, was that he knew people would never have given him the credit he deserved.

He'd have to start all over again, right from the beginning, which is to say from birth. It didn't matter what he turned his hand to: he could have been number one. That's what he'd have to tell them—among other things. Because it was the truth. As a boy, he'd been the best at every sport. When he saw someone struggling to pick up some skill, he'd say, "There's nothing to it, you know." And without even practicing, just by doing it, he was able to master whatever it was on first try.

As to his years with his own family—perhaps that was what people were going to get most wrong. He hadn't even begun to get the reality across.

For one thing, they'd accuse him of never having loved his wife and children, which was totally off the mark.

He loved them *well enough*—that was it! He did what he had to. He was what people call a good father. No one could find fault with him when it came to that.

Deep down, he'd always done his best. He'd tried hard to be an ordinary sort of person, conventional, well behaved, decent. He'd spared neither time nor trouble.

His children were well fed, well dressed, well housed.

Each of them had their own room, though they shared a bathroom. That wasn't the case in most families. When it came to the upkeep of the household, he'd never shortchanged anyone.

So the thing was, you can do everything you're supposed to do and still find yourself alone in a corner, feeling confused, feeling like there must be something more to life, that maybe there had been something else you could have done!

That was what he had to make them understand. At night, when Frida—it seemed funny, now, saying her name—when Frida did her homework, when Mother pasted her pictures into her album, and he fiddled with the radio while smoking his cigar, he couldn't keep himself from feeling alone.

And then, when he'd heard the train whistle, only a few hundred yards from the house . . .

Meanwhile, he walked—through streets that were dark and through streets that were too bright. Sometimes he ran into groups of revelers. Their arms were linked and they wore paper hats, like the members of the local counsel.

He met men who shuffled along, picking up cigarette butts from the sidewalk, who stopped in front of cafés, vaguely hoping for something. He passed cops who were spending their New Year's Eve on a street corner, halfheartedly watching over the city.

He knew that because they didn't even give him a second look!

He would write his memoirs. In fact, he'd already tried to start, just that morning. But he hadn't been up to it. To write he had to have a room of his own.

And yet the moment he was by himself, his ideas dried up, or rather his thoughts took a different turn, and he found himself longing to look at himself in a mirror—to see if something about his face had changed.

Writing in a café would suit him better. There you got a whiff of other people's lives like the whiff of a roaring stove. Except for one thing: if he were to ask for paper and pen now, the waiter was sure to raise an eyebrow, sneak off to the telephone, call the cops.

What exactly *did* he have the right to do anymore? Hard to

say, since Commissioner Lucas wasn't saying anything to the papers or may have ordered them to keep quiet.

He couldn't take a train, in any case. That was for sure. There was no way that a cop wasn't posted in every station, keeping an eye on the passengers going by with Kees Popinga's description in mind.

Girls? He still didn't know. He'd have to try, but it was a big risk. Then again, if he went on sleeping alone, he knew he was going to have terrible nights. Which would have a terrible effect on him the next day. From the moment he got up, he'd feel sluggish; his head wouldn't be as clear as it usually was.

What he really needed was a woman like Jeanne Rozier. She would have understood. She would have helped him. She was smart. And she knew it—he was convinced. She could tell he was different from that gigolo, Louis, who was good for nothing except stealing cars and unloading them out of town, which was child's play. The proof was that Popinga had known how to do it the very first time he'd tried. He hadn't even batted an eye!

Had the cops taken his tip? Were they watching the garage in Juvisy? Who could know? He hadn't acted arbitrarily. Louis was behind bars. No doubt he'd be there for a few years, along with Goin and the others. Jeanne Rozier would be on her own, and then . . .

Meanwhile he had to find somewhere to sleep. The problem was becoming excruciating, and every night it was there again, with all the attendant risks. Kees wasn't sure just where he was. He had to check the street signs and locate a Métro station before he figured out he was on the boulevard Pasteur. It was a part of town he'd never been to before. It didn't seem any better than the Gobelins.

There were lights still on in some of the apartments. People were heading out and looking for taxis after spending the evening with friends. One couple was arguing and as he went by he heard the woman saying, "Even if it was New Year's Eve, you didn't have to ask her to dance so often..."

What a weird life! What a weird night! An old man was stretched out on a bench, asleep. Two cops walked by with measured step. No doubt they were discussing their pay.

Getting used to sleeping alone was going to be hard work ... But he hadn't realized at the time ... And now he felt annoyance, thinking about the fat girl in blue satin he'd clasped in his arms ... Seedy and sordid as it was, he'd gotten into the habit of this nightly intimacy with a stranger.

Why not go ahead? Why not one more time? True, there weren't a lot of girls out alone on this particular night. He didn't see any in their usual haunts in front of the hotels. Maybe they were celebrating the new year, too?

He kept going. From a distance, he glimpsed the Montparnasse station. He didn't go closer. The place had to be dangerous.

Half an hour later he still hadn't found anyone. His legs were tired and he was in a terrible mood, and he went into a hotel hoping that maybe he'd find a chambermaid there. An old night clerk, who was in just as bad a mood as he was, sat at the reception desk. Since Kees didn't have any baggage, he had to pay in advance to get the key.

Worse, his watch had stopped. He had no idea what time it was when he finally fell asleep or when he woke up, and because the room was over a courtyard, there was no way to tell from the street traffic.

Only when he was outside did he realize how early it was. The city was as deserted and gloomy as always after a holiday. Nothing but people from the suburbs, all dressed up, emerging from the train stations offering their best wishes. The day was gray and an icy wind swept the streets. It was more like All Saints' than New Year's.

At least he'd be able to learn the psychiatrists' diagnoses of him from the newspaper. He unfolded it as he was walking down the street that lead to the military college.

In spite of its being a holiday, Professor Abram extended a warm welcome to us last evening. He had given only a cursory reading to Kees Popinga's letter and wished to study it at greater length. However, he summed up his initial impression in one word: in his opinion, the Dutchman is a paranoiac. If his pride is sufficiently wounded, he could prove to be extremely dangerous, all the more so because people of this type remain astonishingly self-controlled under all circumstances.

Professor Linze will be away from Paris for another few days. He will deliver his opinion as soon as he returns.

The police report no new developments. Commissioner Lucas was busy all day yesterday with a narcotics investigation. His colleagues continue to work on the Popinga case.

Progress is being made, sources say, though the quai des Orfèvres refuses to comment.

For now, we can only report that it does not appear that Popinga will be at large much longer.

Why?—he was talking to himself—yes, why wouldn't he be at large much longer? And why didn't they provide any details? Why were they calling him—what was it?—a paranoiac?

He'd heard the word, of course, even if he wasn't exactly sure what it meant. Couldn't they have defined it somehow? If only he could look it up in a dictionary! But where was he supposed to find one? In Groningen you had to sign your name in a register to get into the public library. It must be the same in Paris.

In cafés you could ask for the phone book or a train schedule, but it wasn't likely that they kept a dictionary handy for the customers' use.

The whole thing was rotten! As if, out of sheer maliciousness, they were trying to cast some kind of spell. There was, for one thing, that mention of progress that was being made but that no one would talk about!

Jeanne Rozier knew the commissioner, and she'd said, hadn't she, that he was a bad man? Popinga was once again starting to feel that this cop wasn't putting himself to any trouble. He wasn't even looking for him, that's how sure he was that his victim was going to trip up all on his own.

From the way he came off in the papers, and from the few ambiguous remarks he'd deigned to make, wasn't that how it looked?

Lucas was making a mistake, though. Popinga had no plans at all to run headlong into a trap! He was at least as smart as that fine fellow, not to mention the other one, the shrink, that big shot, with his one word: "Paranoiac!"

Like the others who called him a "nutcase" or a "fiend," or the Montmartre woman who had said he was "sad"! Or the thin girl on the rue de Birague in whose opinion he "only liked them plump"!

He knew who he was, and that was what made him their superior.

He found an old-fashioned café where the walls were covered in tile. He drank a coffee and ate a croissant and reread the article. It was far too short. Then he remembered the girl in blue satin. He looked everywhere before turning up a few lines in the News in Brief:

In the course of a New Year's party in the Gobelins last night, a spurned lover, Jean R——, fired a bullet in the direction of Germaine H——, the daughter of a wine merchant who is a highly regarded member of the local council. Fortunately, no one was seriously injured. Germain V—— was grazed by the bullet while dancing, but was able to return home after treatment. Jean R—— was taken into custody...

Kees laughed out loud, he didn't know why. It was hilarious, the drama ending like that, though probably it would continue and conclude in a wedding. Because Popinga wasn't at all sure that Germaine H—— hadn't, as people say, wanted it to happen.

All that remained was to see if Julius de Coster had answered his ad, since he'd probably continued to read the *Morning Post* on a daily basis. Popinga caught a bus. He'd have to go more than halfway across Paris to reach the post office on the rue de Berri. He went to General Delivery and without hesitation handed over his two envelopes addressed to Smitson.

They didn't ask any questions. They looked through the "S's," and handed him a letter. The address was typewritten.

He retreated to a corner to open it. It felt thick. First he drew out four one-pound notes, then there was a piece of paper with a few lines on it, also typewritten.

I'm sorry I can't send more. New beginnings are always difficult and this is the most I can spare right now. Keep me informed as necessary and I'll do everything I can to help.

J.

That was all. To think that Julius de Coster wasn't the least bit astonished by Popinga's deeds! To think that no one was— that all they could find to sum up his case was a single senseless word: "Paranoiac"!

Though Mother—it was true—had hit upon "amnesia." All by herself!

10

In which Kees Popinga changes shirts while the police and fate, disdaining all the rules of the game, join in a wicked conspiracy.

No, HE wasn't losing heart. That would make all those fine upstanding people all too happy. But when he opened the paper or saw the headlines at a newsstand, he couldn't help but suppress a bitter smile.

They gave him no credit at all—they didn't bother to acknowledge the guts with which he was playing the game, that it was him alone against everyone else, and that under the circumstances, going about his everyday life was anything but easy.

He changed his shirts in café bathrooms. When you were living on the run, cafés were important places. The first time he'd come out with his old shirt in hand. He got rid of it by dropping it in the public urinal.

And he almost got caught! A policeman had seen it happen. As soon as Kees walked out of the urinal, the cop went in—so fast that Popinga broke into a run.

Now it was time to change his shirt again, and he figured the best thing would be to toss the old one into the Seine. But it was sure to be harder than you'd think to do it without being seen. At the last moment, some fisherman or drunk, a pair of lovers or a woman walking her dog would inevitably happen along...

And who suspected anything about this whole other dimension to his life? Not the papers, at any rate. He'd given them something to write about and free copy too. Never mind that not one had spared him a shred of sympathy.

Not that he was asking them to come right out and say they were on his side. He wasn't asking for two daily columns on the front page, either. But he wasn't an idiot. There are ways of presenting things that are sympathetic and ways that are not. And in France, in the News in Brief, the attitude was always sympathetic.

Except when it came to him. And why was that? It had to be Commissioner Lucas's doing. What else?

He hadn't robbed anyone, which should have reassured the middle classes. If Pamela was dead, that had been a mistake. And both times he'd attacked a certain kind of girl, which should have laid the fears of all decent women to rest.

Landru had a multitude of crimes on his conscience and was ugly to boot, but half the public was behind him!

How come? And how come there was this undeclared hostility toward him in the papers? When they weren't giving him the silent treatment, they featured nothing but uninteresting facts:

We had promised to furnish our readers with Doctor Linze's opinion on the case of the fleeing Dutchman. The doctor informs us that he would like to be of assistance, but that offering a diagnosis on the basis of a single letter would, in his view, be inappropriate—especially in light of the gravity of the situation.

That's what it had come to! His person, life, and liberty had become a mere side story. The next day, Professor Abram, who clearly felt that he had been impugned by his colleague, responded:

> A comment has been falsely attributed to me in relation to a matter that would otherwise hardly merit discussion. Speaking freely, I may have gone so far as to suggest that Kees Popinga could be considered a textbook paranoiac. It was in no way my intention, however, to offer this entirely provisional opinion as an actual diagnosis.

Even the psychiatrists seemed to have had enough of him! While Saladin, the reporter who, at the beginning, had written the best pieces, wasn't even bothering to byline his updates! Popinga didn't know Saladin. He had no idea if he was young or old, happy or unhappy. Still, his betrayal was depressing.

Why even bother to publish such dreary stuff?

> Without breaking for the holidays, a team of expert accountants has been reviewing the ledgers of Julius de Coster and Son. In a just-released preliminary report, they declare that it will be several more weeks before their work is complete. The situation of the firm appears to be considerably worse than first thought. It is now a question not only of a serious financial collapse, but also of fraud.
>
> In other news, the Wilhelmina Canal has been dragged for several days to no avail. The body of Julius de Coster has not been found. The possibility that it has been carried out to sea by a ship has been ruled out.
>
> The general assumption is that this is a case of a staged suicide and that the ship owner has fled the country.

What did any of it have to do with Popinga? On the other hand, a malicious pleasure lay behind the publication of such articles as:

> Commissioner Lucas traveled to Lyon yesterday as part of an ongoing investigation. He declined to say, however, whether his trip was connected to the Popinga case or that of a drug gang, several members of which are already behind bars.

Why Lyon? And why did they keep coming back to the story of this gang that nobody cared about? Some invisible agency seemed to be at work—bent on breaking all the rules of the game.

And who else could it be but Commissioner Lucas? One way or another, he was preventing the reporters from pursuing their usual investigations.

Because in the normal course of events all the papers would be following their own leads. They would have their own theories and clues. They'd be interviewing people and publishing what they'd found out.

And yet no one had even thought about approaching Jeanne Rozier! Not a word about her condition! She might be fine now and back working at Picratt's—it was impossible to say. Not a word about Louis, either. There'd been no mention of his return from Marseille.

It was harassment, deliberate harassment. What other way was there to look at it? It was impossible to believe that somebody or other hadn't seen Popinga and told the police. If so, why the silence?

They were trying to push him to the limit, of course! He knew all about that. He shrugged. He let out a sigh of contempt. He could tell they were trying to shut him in behind a wall of silence.

Never mind that he was keeping a tight grip on things. When he walked the streets, he made sure that he never confronted passersby with a quizzical glance or an ironic one. He stayed away from prostitutes, preferring to sleep badly or to stay awake half the night, even with his heart pounding.

And he'd just made a new discovery. Because he'd figured it was a good idea to keep varying the places he stayed at, he'd ended up one night in Javel at a really seedy hotel. It was a mistake. He wasn't dressed appropriately for such a dive. The people had been openmouthed with astonishment.

Don't sink too low, then, and don't try to climb too high! Then again, he only had twelve hundred francs left; one of these days he'd have to come up with some more money. It was something to think about. But there was still time; he'd have to examine the question.

It was the night of January 7 that he'd spent in Javel. After that he'd thrown his dirty shirt in the Seine and headed across town to read the newspapers. It was raining. For others, that was nothing—a minor inconvenience. But for him—since he had to spend the better part of his day on the streets and since he didn't have a change of clothes—for him it mattered. Rain was like one of nature's dirty tricks.

And what a dirty trick!

He was in a nice place not far from the Madeleine, reading the paper that featured Saladin's articles, when he saw the headline POLICE RELEASE CAR THIEF, and he couldn't help it—he exploded with laughter.

The thing was, for days he'd been expecting something of the sort. He hadn't been wrong to think that something fishy was up. But to imagine that...

At 5 PM yesterday, the head of the gang of car thieves arrested last week was released from police headquarters.

Louis emerged from the office of Police Commissioner Lucas. There was no official explanation.

The following conjectures are therefore based entirely on our ongoing private investigation.

Commissioner Lucas personally directed the arrest of the car thieves on the night of January 1—a highly unusual procedure. No announcement of the arrest was made to the press.

What accounts for this silence? Why have there been no further developments in a case of such significance, with four men and a woman behind bars?

This same Louis is the leader of the "Juvisy gang," named after the location of the garage where the stolen cars were processed. From this clue we can deduce answers to the questions posed above.

Louis is a former cocaine dealer and the lover of a certain Jeanne Rozier.

Readers will recall that Jeanne Rozier...

Kees Popinga could have done a better job with the rest of the article than his friend Saladin. He smiled. He was brimming over with contempt for the press, for Lucas, for all humanity!

The link explains Commissioner Lucas's personal involvement in the Juvisy arrests. The gang members included a former brothel-maid, Rose, and her brother Goin, who owns the garage. The suspects were questioned. Once again the press was not notified.

In our opinion, it is highly unlikely that Louis's release amounts to an exoneration. His activities are widely known, even if the quai des Orfèvres chooses to remain silent. A well-informed source explains, "If Louis is out on the street, it's because he's got a job to do."

Louis has since been sighted making the rounds in the cafés frequented by his usual associates. He is said to bear a message from the police.

Not to put too fine a point on it, Kees Popinga, the assailant of Jeanne Rozier, is not only being sought by the whole police force. He is being sought by a gang. That gang wants his skin.

Only an accident can forestall his imminent arrest...

Popinga was looking at himself in the mirror across the room. All the blood had drained from his face. His lips were incapable of forming a smile, no matter how sarcastic.

So all his fears were confirmed! He felt a lot friendlier to Saladin now. Without him, he would have been completely in the dark. He would have gone on his way without the slightest suspicion of the plot that was being hatched against him.

It was simple, goddammit! He pulled off the Juvisy caper, and the gang had been arrested. But Lucas had known better than to shout it from the rooftops. He'd gone to the newspapers and kept them happy with a bunch of stories about drugs.

And now he must have shown Kees's letter to Louis. Obviously he hadn't thought twice about striking some kind of dirty deal.

So that was it! The cops had made a deal with Louis! The police had let him out so he could settle his score with Popinga! In other words, they weren't capable of catching him on their own!

Kees had been full of contempt and anger before; now he felt a deep, undying disgust. He asked for paper and took out his pen, but when he was about to write he gave up with a feeble shrug of his shoulders. Who was he going to write to? Saladin? Telling him his article had it right? To Commissioner Lucas, with sarcastic congratulations? Who? And what was the point?

Now that Louis was part of the hunt, they thought they'd won and they were saying as much. Now all the whores and johns in Paris, not to mention the front desk of every dive and flophouse, would be on the lookout, eager to turn him in.

The police had never laid eyes on him, but Louis had.

"Waiter! What do I owe?"

He paid the tab but he didn't leave. He didn't really know why. He'd walked back and forth across Paris so many times— suddenly he was exhausted. He sat on the moleskin banquette and stared out at the street and the umbrellas parading by.

So that was how it was. A car thief, a crook and a pimp, was officially preferable to him. It was true! Nobody could claim it wasn't. And if Louis pulled it off, no doubt they'd turn a blind eye to the activities of the Juvisy gang!

"Waiter!"

He was thirsty. What the hell! He needed to think, and a drink could only help.

When you came right down to it, it had been a mistake to stop after that business with Jeanne Rozier. He saw that clearly! He was beginning to understand how public opinion worked. On the very next day, they should have picked up their news-papers and read: KEES POPINGA ATTACKS YOUNG WOMAN IN TRAIN. Just like that—something new every day—so as to keep the public waiting with bated breath while he became a legend.

Would they have taken such a passionate interest in Landru if he'd killed just a woman or two?

And maybe, instead of revealing the whole of his thinking, he should have lied in his letter. If, for example, he'd led them to believe that even in Groningen, where he'd been considered such a model citizen, he'd already committed certain unspeci-fied criminal acts.

He reread Saladin's article. It confirmed his suspicions: Louis was now the star of the story, not him. Louis was the lead.

Tomorrow everybody's sympathy would be with him, Jeanne's lover! A manhunt through the Paris underworld, led by a criminal and tacitly sanctioned by the cops—people would eat it up!

No, he wasn't losing heart. He didn't want to and he wasn't going to, not at any price. But he had a right to feel exhausted for a moment, while the enormity of the injustice that had been done to him sank in. How many people were on his trail now? Hundreds? Thousands?

Which wasn't going to stop him from drinking a glass of brandy and watching the rain fall in peace. Let them look! Let them inspect every passerby! A lone man is always stronger than a crowd if he can keep his wits about him. And Popinga wasn't going to lose his cool.

He'd made only one mistake: right from the start, he should have considered the whole world his enemy. Now they didn't take him seriously. They weren't scared. It made perfect sense for them to treat him like a clown.

Paranoiac!

And now? What difference did any of it make? Here he sat, all snug and warm in a nice restaurant, with his second glass of brandy in front of him, and nothing was going to stop him from thumbing his nose or snapping his fingers at the whole of Paris or from doing whatever he made up his mind to do. He was going to decide what this very day—it would be something big, something that would make them all tremble, the car thieves, the whores, Louis's cronies, all of them.

He didn't know yet. He had time. Better not to rush. Better to wait for inspiration to come while he watched the dumb herd of people, all in a row, walking by on the street. Some of them were even running, not that it was going to do them any good. While a cop in a cape—solemn as a pope and with the idea that he was making himself useful—made a point of goofing around with his whistle and white nightstick! Wouldn't it have been a whole lot smarter of him to come over and ask Popinga for his papers, instead of putting on such a show?

Just like that, it would all be over. No more Popinga case, no more need for Louis or any of the others, or for this Commissioner Lucas, who no doubt thought he was about as clever as they come!

But he wasn't all that shrewd. Kees knew that because, even though he'd been in the dark, he'd felt this thing coming for several days now and had forced himself to sleep alone.

But he wasn't so sure he'd be sleeping alone anymore. Maybe not. Who could say? And if he didn't, his companions weren't going to be telling any stories...

The blood rushed to his head. He looked at himself in the mirror again. Was that really what he was thinking? Why not? What was to stop him?

He turned around. Someone was speaking to him in English. The fellow at the neighboring table, who'd been writing for the last several minutes.

"Excuse me, sir," he said, smiling, "you don't happen to speak English?"

"Yes."

"Are you English?"

"Yes."

"In that case, I hope you'll excuse me if I ask a favor. I've just arrived in Paris. From America. I'm trying to find out from the waiter how many stamps to put on this envelope, but he doesn't seem to understand me."

Popinga called the waiter over and translated. He examined the stranger, who was gushing with gratitude while sticking stamps on a letter to New Orleans.

"You're lucky you speak French," the American remarked

as he closed his writing pad. "I've really been at a loss since I arrived. People don't even understand when I ask directions on the street. Do you know Paris?"

"Pretty well, yes."

Funny to think that in just one week he'd covered the whole city.

"Friends gave me the address of a place, a bar run by an American, where all the Americans in Paris go. Do you know it?"

The man wasn't exactly young. He had gray hair, blotchy cheeks, a red nose—you could tell he was somebody with a taste for the hard stuff.

"It seems it's right near the Opéra. I looked for half an hour without any luck."

He took a piece of paper from his large raincoat.

"Rue...wait...rue de la Michodière."

"I know it, yes."

"Is it far?"

"Five minutes' walk."

The other man seemed to hesitate, then said, "How about having a drink with me there? Do you mind? I haven't talked to anyone in two days."

As to Popinga—it was a whole week since he'd last talked to anyone.

Five minutes later the two men were walking down one of the grand boulevards. A street vendor overheard them. He had some attractive postcards.

"What are they?" the Yankee asked.

Kees blushed, "Oh, nothing. Just tourist stuff..."

"Have you lived in Paris for a long time?"

"Pretty long, yes."

"I'm just here for a week before going to Italy, then it's back to New Orleans. Ever been there?"

"No."

People turned to look. They were the tourist type, like the ones who saunter down the grand boulevards, talking in loud voices as if no one understood a word.

Popinga pointed. "There it is—down there."

He was careful not to say anything to the guy that could land him in trouble. He might be with the police or one of Louis's gang. Still, he'd have his work cut out for him.

Kees pushed open the door of the bar. The place was new to him, and he was struck by the atmosphere and decor.

This wasn't France. This was the United States. Big muscular men stood around a high mahogany bar, smoking and drinking and talking loudly. Two bartenders, one Chinese, were busy serving whiskeys and immense glasses of beer. The mirror was all chalked up with inscriptions.

"A whiskey, right?"

"Thanks."

For Popinga it was a change from the restaurants of the last few days. He knew the decor there all too well, the brass-plated ball-shaped lamp stands with cast-iron bases, the little lectern for the phone books, the cashier perched high on a stool, the waiters in their white aprons.

Here, it made you think of something else—a long voyage, a stopover in some faraway country. Kees strained to listen and realized that most of the customers were discussing that afternoon's races. A fat guy, the fattest of them all, with four chins and a brown check coat, was taking bets.

"Are you also in business?" Popinga's new friend asked.

"Yes, the grain business."

He said it because he knew something about the grain trade; the de Costers had been involved in it.

"I'm in leather. Like a sausage? Here—have one! I'm sure they're excellent. We're in America here, and in America they make excellent sausage."

People came, people left. A thick haze of smoke hovered over the bar and the walls were covered with photos of American sports stars, most of them inscribed to the owner.

"It's really a great place, right? The friend who gave me the address said it was the best in Paris. Bartender, two whiskeys!"

He didn't miss a beat; he leered: "Is it true that Frenchwomen like foreign guys so much? I haven't had time to visit swinging Montmartre yet. I guess I'm a little afraid . . ."

"Afraid of what?"

"Back home they say there are a lot of bad characters there, ones who are even sharper than our own—and that foreigners get robbed. Have you ever been robbed?"

"Never. And I go to Montmartre a lot."

"You've picked up women there?"

"Sure."

"Without their having some kind of accomplice hidden in the room?"

Popinga was distracted from the perfidies of Commissioner Lucas. He was the old hand now, who's seen it all and gives advice to the newcomer. The more he studied his companion the more naïve he found him. He was more even naïve than a Dutchman.

"Their friends aren't in the room—they're waiting outside."

"Waiting for what?"

"Nothing. Just waiting. Don't worry."

"Do you bring a gun?"

"Never!"

"When I go to New York on business, I always bring a gun."

"You're in Paris now!"

The sausages were good. Popinga emptied his glass. It was filled again.

"Are you staying at a nice hotel?"

"Very nice."

"Me," the foreign guy said, "I'm at the Grand Hôtel. It's fantastic."

And he offered his cigar case to Kees, who took one out without compunction. After all, it had been a long time. Here especially he could allow himself the luxury of a cigar.

"Do you know where to get American newspapers? I'd like to see how the stock market's doing."

"Any newsstand. There's one down the street, on the corner."

"Do you mind? I'll be right back. Order some more sausages, okay?"

It was one in the afternoon and the place was clearing out; most of the customers had left to have lunch. Popinga waited for five minutes, surprised that his companion wasn't back. Then his thoughts wandered. When he looked at the clock again it was a quarter past.

He hadn't noticed the bartender examining him closely. He didn't see him turn around and say something under his breath to the Chinese guy.

The whiskey'd done him good. He felt more sure of himself. He was still in a position to respond to Lucas and to Louis and he promised himself that, that very afternoon, he'd come up with a plan that would astonish them all and make the newspapers take a different tone when they talked about him.

Why hadn't the American come back? He couldn't have gotten lost! Popinga opened the door and checked the sidewalk outside. He saw the corner newsstand, but there was no sign of his friend.

All he could do was laugh. He'd been taken, no doubt about it. The other guy had stuck him with the bill.

One more disappointment. He was beginning to get used to them.

"I'll have another whiskey."

He'd get drunk. Whatever happened, he was sure he'd never be so dumb as to betray himself. He'd figure out...

With time to kill he tried the gumball machine, then asked for another cigar; he'd dropped his. He looked around. The bar was completely empty. The Chinese guy was having lunch at the opposite end of the room. The other bartender was re-arranging bottles.

All that simply to get him to pay for four sausages and a few whiskeys—how low could you stoop! He wasn't rich by any means. He needed his money more than most. For him, it could be called a question of life and death. One detail that said it all: if he got his shirt dirty, there was no way for him to wash it. He had to buy another and throw the one he'd been wearing into the Seine, even if for all intents and purposes it was as good as new.

Why not order another sausage and skip lunch? And why not spend an afternoon at the track? It would do him good. He was tired of making the same old rounds of the same old places.

He was about to open his mouth. The bartender opened his at the same time, quite by chance, it seemed. Popinga let him speak first.

"Excuse me for asking. Do you know the gentleman you were just with?"

"I know him... a little bit. A little bit, yes."

The bartender was embarrassed. He continued: "Do you know what he does?"

"He's in leather."

The Chinese guy was listening from his seat at the other end of the room. Popinga understood that something was up. He was on the verge of rising and getting out of there as fast as he could.

"So, he took you."

"What do you mean?"

"I was afraid to warn you, because there were people around, then I couldn't tell if you were one of his friends or not." The bartender sighed as he shifted a bottle of gin. "So as it turns out I guess I've been had too."

"I don't understand!"

"I know. But you will soon enough. Did you have a lot of money on you?"

"Enough."

"Look for your wallet. I don't know what pocket you carry it in, but I'll bet you anything it's gone."

Popinga patted himself and felt his throat tighten. It was just as the bartender had said: his wallet was no longer in his pocket!

"You didn't notice that all the time he was talking he kept touching you? He's a professional. I've known him for ten years. The cops, too. He's one of the best pickpockets in Europe."

For a second, Popinga had closed his eyes. His hand felt around in his overcoat...

It wasn't enough that the American had stolen all his money, the only thing that allowed him to fight back, but he'd also made off with his razor—fooled, no doubt, by the shape of its box. He must have mistaken it for a carrying case.

Today alone, thousands of people in Paris would have fallen victim to similar thefts. But for most of them, if not all, the loss of cash would have been more or less unimportant.

But for one man and one alone, for Kees Popinga, those twelve hundred francs and that razor were, you could say, salvation itself. He was more vulnerable than anybody else. Fate, in the form of a newspaper article, had turned on him that morning wearing an ugly look.

But he'd hoped it would hold off; he'd looked for a kind of break. He'd taken the whiskeys, the sausages, the talk. They were a change from his unending monologue.

"I almost warned you. But at first you never looked in my

direction. So I thought you might be a friend of his, like I said, even his partner."

The bartender went on apologizing. Popinga smiled agreeably.

"Was it a lot that you lost?"

"No. Not a lot," Kees said. The same almost angelic smile lingered on his face.

Because it wasn't a lot or a little that he'd lost. It was everything. Everything a man can lose, out of stupidity or from bad luck, because luck was toying with him just as the cops were and just as Louis was too!

He couldn't make up his mind to leave. He lowered his head because he felt his eyes growing hot. He was afraid of the tears welling up in his eyes.

It was too much! Too stupid! Too unbelievable!

"Do you live a long way off?"

He smiled. He actually smiled. He had the strength for that.

"Far enough, yes."

"Listen. I trust you. I'll lend you twenty francs for a taxi. I don't know if you're thinking of filing a report with the cops. If they caught him, at any rate, that would be best for everyone."

He nodded yes. He wanted to sit and think, his head in his hands, maybe burst out laughing or into sobs. It wasn't just stupid—it was disgusting, and in his mind he knew he didn't deserve it.

What had he done? Yes, what had he done? Except...

Except for a little thing, obviously, but it had seemed fair enough to him. And he hadn't been thinking, in any case. It was because of his hatred of Rose, his blind hatred, because there was nothing he could hold against her...He'd written to Commissioner Lucas; he'd turned in the whole gang...

Was it because of that—a kind of aftereffect?

He took the twenty francs the bartender was holding out to him. Raising his eyes, he saw his face in the mirror, splintered by the white chalk inscriptions, a face that expressed nothing, not pain and not despair, nothing at all, a face that looked like another he'd once seen, some ten years ago, in Groningen, the face of a man who'd been run over by a train and whose legs had been neatly severed... He was wounded, but he hadn't realized it yet. There hadn't been enough time for him to feel the agony. And while people around him fainted, he looked at them in total surprise, wondering what was the matter with them, what was the matter with him, why he was there, on the ground, in the middle of a screaming crowd.

"Excuse me," he stammered. "Thanks."

He opened the door... and walked. Or he must have, but he wasn't aware of it, or of the direction he went in, or of the people he brushed against, or of talking to himself out loud...

Cheating! That was the truth and the only truth, loud and clear! They were cheating! They were cheating because he was too strong, because they couldn't beat him any other way, not fairly!

Commissioner Lucas was the worst of all. He was afraid to have his picture printed in the papers! And he wasn't ashamed of a cheap bluff, like letting people think he was in Lyon and that he didn't know anything about the car thieves.

Louis was cheating and making deals with the police. Jeanne Rozier too...

Popinga would never have believed it of her. The others provoked his contempt, his indignation; she hurt him. He'd always felt that there was something between them.

The proof was that he hadn't killed her.

Even fate was cheating him—sending this trashy American who couldn't do anything except empty somebody's pockets. What use was a sixteen-franc razor to him?

It was just too stupid for words.

It was plain rotten.

II

How Kees Popinga learns that it costs sixty francs to dress up like a drunken bum; how he prefers to go naked.

THINKING might be even more exhausting than walking—especially since Popinga had some serious thinking to do. He was going to get to the bottom of things, proceed from A to Z, review everything, however remote or near, that pertained to him.

That contemptible Commissioner Lucas and that nobody Louis—together they'd decided—hadn't they—that he would never again have a moment's peace. And an obliging pickpocket had deprived him of the means to sit down.

Because in Paris it costs money to sit down. By five in the afternoon, Kees had been reduced to going into a church in order to think. A bunch of tapers flickered at the feet of a saint he'd never heard of. After which his memory was a blank. Nothing mattered. What mattered was that he was thinking, even if at one point he noticed a passerby looking his way, which brought his thoughts to a screeching halt as Kees himself did a double take and was about to run for dear life. It took all his willpower and cost no end of trouble for him to recover his wits.

Or else he'd find himself distracted from the main thread.

Some insignificant thought would graft itself onto another and then grow and grow until it assumed an entirely senseless importance.

But the endless hours he'd spent walking—they were his problem and his alone. There was no reason anybody else should care, especially since he wasn't about to complain. The fact was, he no longer had the right to stop walking. His twenty francs weren't enough for a hotel and the late-night restaurants were just the place where he'd be most likely to get caught.

If only he was dressed in rags then he could have taken shelter under a bridge. But his clothes were too high quality for a bum. He'd attract suspicion.

He walked, since nobody pays attention to people who are walking and appear to have some place to go. Only there was nowhere for him to go, and from time to time, when he was sure that he was all alone, he would stop to sit on a stoop.

Where were his thoughts taking him? Because some new thought or feeling was always coming up, leading him ever farther astray.

It was like the birth of his daughter, Frida!

How so? It would have been hard for him to say. He'd wandered very far along the Seine; by now he might have even left Paris behind. There were immense factories on the banks of the river. Their windows were all ablaze; their smokestacks lit up the sky with a halo of fire.

The rain came slanting down. Perhaps that was it—when his daughter was born it had been raining too. It had been summer then, but with the same crosshatching of rain. And it must have been just about this time of day. No—because it was summer and the sun came up earlier. But so what! Day hadn't really broken yet and Popinga had gone for a walk in front of the house, in the rain, his head bare, his hands in his pockets, peering up at the second-floor windows. Over in the working-class part of town, across the bridge, there were other windows and other lights. He imagined people who were barely awake, beginning to wash...

What did any of that have to do with him? He had an important decision to make and here he was allowing himself to daydream. He'd even stopped to gaze at the river, which appeared to divide here because there was a canal leading off.

After that the banks were deserted again. Then came tall, gloomy-looking houses where the lights were coming on, a restaurant whose shivering owner was starting the espresso machine.

He shrugged. Always the same old thing. Obviously he could go in, casually walk up to the counter, and—when the owner turned his back—hit him over the head and run off with the cash in the register.

But you didn't need to be Kees Popinga for that.

No! It was hardly worth thinking about. He'd gone over everything in the afternoon, considered all the possibilities, and now it was like a blackboard wiped clean.

It was too late. In fact, it had always been too late—right from the very start.

He was smarter than Landru, smarter than all the rest, the ones everyone talked about, who were famous for their ex-ploits. But those others had been ready, they'd had time to make plans. He could have too, he supposed, if he'd wanted.

Still, it wasn't his fault. If Pamela hadn't laughed so hysteri-cally... Apart from that, he was convinced he hadn't made any mistakes. One day everybody would have to admit it too.

Groups of men passed by on their way to the big factory. Popinga had to be careful not to attract attention. He no longer had the right to get caught.

He had work to do... Afterwards, things would happen

quickly... But, meanwhile, he had to be careful, avoid betraying himself at any cost...

But it's hard not to attract attention when you've been out walking in the rain for ten hours.

Better to keep walking, through Ivry and then Alfortville. It was still dark. The sun didn't begin to rise until he found himself on the banks of the Seine in what seemed to be the country. He noticed mooring posts too.

The water was yellow and the current was running fast, carrying branches and other flotsam. A hundred yards away there was a seedy-looking house. The lights on the bottom floor were on. Popinga saw a sign over the entrance: THE LAUGHING CARP. He had to work to figure it out and when he did, he had to shrug... Fish have small mouths. That was why it was funny for them to laugh!

The house was surrounded by trellises, or rather by cast-iron poles that must have supported trellises in the summer. A dozen boats were hauled up on the bank.

Popinga assumed a look of indifference as he walked by to examine things. He saw a woman tending the stove. A man— no doubt the owner—was sitting at a table covered with oilcloth and tearing a piece of bread off a loaf.

Kees made up his mind. Looking as cheery as he could, he walked in and said in a loud voice, "Nasty weather, isn't it?"

The woman jumped. He was sure he'd scared her, that she'd felt the threat of violence. And yet she looked at him disdainfully and sat back down next to the stove.

"Can a person get a cup of coffee?" he asked.

"Of course."

A cat lay on a chair. It had rolled itself into a ball.

"And what about a little bread and butter too?"

These people didn't know who they were dealing with. They suspected even less that by tomorrow...

He ate, though he wasn't hungry. Then the sun came up and they turned off the electric lights. He asked for something to write with.

So there he was seated in front of some cheap graph paper of the sort found in village groceries. He looked out the window at a dreary stretch of river and wrote:

To the Editor in Chief,

As your newspaper reported yesterday, a certain Commissioner Lucas, who for the last two weeks has been saying my arrest is only a matter of hours, has released some common criminals and felons and set them on my trail.

Would you be so good as to print this letter? It will put an end to a pointless pursuit, not to mention to a situation that is bereft of both glory and honor.

This is the last time I will write or ever be heard from. Which is to say, I have found a way to achieve the goal I set for myself when I left Groningen and broke all the accepted rules.

By the time you receive this letter, my name will no longer be Kees Popinga, nor will I be in the position of a criminal on the lam.

My name will be respected, my position in life unchallenged. I will be one of those individuals for whom everything is permitted—because they have money and are without scruple.

Forgive me if I maintain silence about my base of activities, whether London, America, or even Paris. Discretion, you understand, is indispensable.

Suffice it to say I will be an important man. Instead of dealing with Pamelas or Jeanne Roziers, I will choose stars of the stage and the screen for my official mistresses.

That, sir, is what I wanted to communicate. I have

reserved this exclusive for you because yesterday's article by your reporter Saladin was very helpful to me.

Let me say again—and I know what I'm talking about! —that by the time you receive this letter, I will be utterly out of reach. M. Lucas will have to drop the investigation he has conducted so far with such brilliance and style.

Thus I will have demonstrated how, simply by virtue of his intelligence, one man, who may have been nothing more than a lackey back when he obeyed the rules of the game, can rise to whatever level he chooses, once he has regained his freedom.

Please accept, dear sir, the warmest greetings of one who for the last time signs himself as,

Kees Popinga

A sense of irony almost led him to add "paranoiac." Then, since the owner was standing by the glass-paned door, watching the rain fall, and since Popinga could see the little green-painted boats, he felt the need to say, "I own a boat, too."

"Ah," said the man politely.

"Only it's very different. I don't think you have them here in France."

He explained the construction of his boat while the woman carried in some buckets to clean up.

But what was strange was the way his eyes pricked as soon as he began to talk about the Zeedeufel. He had to look away. He saw his boat, bobbing like a toy at the edge of the canal, and then . . .

"What do I owe? By the way . . . How do I get to Paris?"

"There's the tram—five hundred yards from here."

"And is it far to Juvisy?"

"You'd have to catch a train at Alfortville. Or go to Paris and take the bus."

It was hard to go. He looked at the table where he'd been writing, at the stove, at the cat basking in the heat on the straw chair, at the old woman getting down on her knees to wash the floor, at the man smoking his curved pipe and wearing a blue sailor's sweater.

"The Laughing Carp," he said to himself.

He would have liked to have said something to them, to let them know that, without being aware of it, they'd witnessed an event of the first importance. He wanted to tell them to read tomorrow's papers.

He loitered. He would have liked a drink too, but he had to hold on to his twenty francs.

"I'm leaving," he said with a sigh.

Which was all the man and the woman were waiting for. To them he seemed strange.

He'd had a different idea at first. He'd go to Juvisy on foot, following the Seine. There was no reason to hurry since he had the whole day ahead. But while he was writing he changed his mind, proving just how self-possessed he continued to be. Because if his letter was postmarked from some place near Juvisy, they'd connect the dots; his missive would be pointless.

Better to go back to Paris. He took the tram. It vibrated so much that on top of his exhaustion he felt sick. Near the Louvre he bought a stamp. He found a mailbox and held the letter on the edge of the drop for a good long time before letting it fall into the void.

From now on, there was no need to think. It would be enough to execute point by point the plan that he'd devised—making no mistakes.

It was still raining. Paris was gray, dirty, and confused—a nightmare. It was crammed with people who had no idea where they were going; crammed with streets, the ones around les Halles where people slipped on rotting vegetables; crammed with shop windows that were crammed with shoes. It was the first time he'd noticed all the shoe stores, the hundreds and hundreds of pairs on their shelves.

His letter could have also said . . .

No! For it to be believable, he had to leave some things out. In any case, it was too late! Too late for everything! He hadn't even had the guts to take the guy's clothes!

Because he needed clothes, no matter what. And one night, somewhere, not far from where the Métro crossed over a bridge, he'd stumbled on a drunk who was asleep on a bench.

He could have hit him over the head and stripped him of his clothes. That was all it took and what harm could it do? The man had vomited. There was an empty bottle at his side.

Popinga was sure that he hadn't felt any pity. That wasn't it. Only he understood that it was too late—nothing more.

And even if he had started off on the right foot, by now he knew things would never have worked out. An article in one of the papers soon supplied the key to the whole drama. Kees had read it, but taken no notice. He'd stuffed it into his pockets along with others of no interest.

"It is obvious that we are dealing with an amateur," the writer said. The byline was "Charles Bélières."

But he understood now! He'd understood as soon as the bartender told him that his wallet had been stolen. *He was an amateur!* That was why Commissioner Lucas treated him with such contempt, why the papers failed to take him seriously, why Louis and his gang were out looking for him.

An amateur! It had been up to him, and him alone, to prove otherwise. But to do that he would have had to have taken action earlier, and, above all, done things differently . . .

It was all over—so why was he still trying to think? He should give up. He already had an upset stomach. This was giving him an upset mind. And he mustn't forget the clothes.

Which was why he had to find his way back to a street he'd stumbled onto the week before, behind the municipal bank, where they sold secondhand things.

He waded through a strange neighborhood, crossing the rue des Rosiers, which somehow reminded him of Jeanne—what would she say to that? Then he had an inspiration: he'd sell his watch. There was no point, though. How much could a watch be worth that he'd picked up for a mere eighty-five francs?

He shouldn't be so touchy. He shouldn't act so forlorn at the sight of a restaurant like a child who's been refused candy. Alcohol wouldn't change anything. What mattered was his letter. He reviewed it in his mind, repeating the sentences. In the end he decided it wasn't so bad, even if he'd left a few things out.

What would they make of it? What sort of comment would it provoke?

Above all, he had to stop looking at himself in shop windows. It was ridiculous. It could attract attention. And, above all, it would end up by making him feel sorry for himself.

He had to walk. There! Now he was on the rue Blancs-Manteaux. He'd noticed the little store on the right last week.

The important thing was to take it easy. He forced himself to smile.

"Excuse me."

Inside the shop an old woman was standing among piles of clothing.

"I'd like to know...I was thinking of dressing up as a bum for a costume party. That would be pretty funny, don't you think?"

He saw himself in a bamboo-framed mirror. Popinga. He was very pale, perhaps because he was tired.

"How much for an old suit like this?"

It was even more worn out than the one that Mother used to donate to some poor old fellow in Groningen every Easter.

"You can have it for fifty francs. It's still in pretty good shape... the lining is new."

That was one of the great surprises of his life. He'd never thought an old suit like that could cost so much. A pair of broken-down shoes would set him back another twenty francs.

"Thanks. I'll think it over. I'll be back..."

She caught up with him in the street. "Come on," she said. "Since it's you, I'll let you have it all for sixty francs. And I'll throw in a cap for free."

Bent low to the ground, he fled. He didn't have sixty francs. He didn't have fifty. He'd make do some other way. He had something in mind already, even if it prompted a bitter smile. This time things were bad beyond belief. It was all thanks to fate.

He'd go all the way. He'd follow through on his idea until reason itself was at an end!

"Too bad for..."

He caught himself in time. He no longer had a right to talk to himself in the street. Having made it this far, it would've been stupid to get caught.

He walked. He went into another church, where they were celebrating a wedding. He thought he'd better leave.

"You idiot! Can't you see where you're going?"

He was the idiot. He'd almost been run over by that car. But Kees didn't even turn around!

And wouldn't it perhaps be just as well to let himself be caught? He'd refuse a lawyer. He'd stand straight as a rod in court. He'd be calm and dignified. He'd open a file, speak softly, "You all thought..."

Too late! The struggle not to backslide was endless. By tonight, his notebook would be in the newspaper's hands. Their first thought would be to turn it over to Commissioner Lucas.

He felt strangely tired—it was like a hangover. His head was clear and at the same time not. The passersby seemed mere shadows; he bumped into them, stammered out excuses, hurried on. Still, he knew every detail of his plan. He found his way without any trouble to the Porte d'Italie, where he looked up the schedule and fares of the buses to Juvisy.

He had eight francs fifty left over after buying his ticket. He wondered if he should eat something or have a drink, and ended up by ordering two croissants and a coffee. He followed them with a shot of hard liquor. Now there was no question of going back—no question of eating or drinking, ever again.

No one suspected a thing. The waiter treated him like any other customer. Someone even asked him for a light.

Around five in the afternoon, he sat on the bus with people who hadn't the slightest idea of what was going on.

And yet only a few days earlier, when he still had money, he could have brought a bomb onto the bus, sat down, and, if he'd wanted to, blown the whole thing to kingdom come. He could have derailed a train! There was nothing to it.

If he was here, now, it was because he wanted to be. Because he had come to the conclusion that it was too late. And because in the end he'd hit upon a better solution.

Everyone would be insane with rage! As for Jeanne Rozier... Who knows? He'd always thought that without quite realizing it she was in love with him. It would be even more true now. Louis was going to look utterly mediocre.

He recognized the steep hill, the houses at the edge of Juvisy. He got out of the bus, but his legs were so weak that he had to rest for a moment before walking on.

One thing puzzled him. He noticed that the lights were on the floor above Goin and Boret's garage. Had they let Goin go, too, then? Unlikely. The papers would have said something about it. And if Goin was there, the lights in the garage should have been on as well.

No! It had to be Rose, no doubt about it. They must have

released her on her own recognizance. That thought nearly ruined everything, because Popinga had to resist his desire to go in, to give her a fright and maybe...

But if he did that, nothing at all would be left—not the letter, not any of the rest! Likewise, he had no right to go back to the café where he'd played the slot machine. The windows were all steamed up, but inside he could see railway workers in uniform.

Perhaps it had been a mistake to eat. It wasn't a big deal. Still, his stomach was upset. He slipped through the empty streets and took an overpass around the station. In the distance, illuminated, he saw the window of his room, the one through which he'd escaped from the garage.

He had to hurry. Otherwise he might lose his nerve. The time was irrelevant, so long as it was dark. The first thing to do was find the Seine, but Popinga realized that he had an inaccurate picture of the lay of the land. No matter how far down the tracks he walked, the river still didn't come into sight.

He crossed empty fields, kitchen gardens, and some abandoned sand pits where he nearly stumbled into a ditch full of water. It seemed to take forever, maybe because he was so tired. Still, he could tell how far he'd come from the clusters of lights indicating villages and housing lots.

Trains passed. He gave a start and looked away. "There's nothing to it, right?" he murmured.

He wiped his eyes as if it was raining. He could taste the salt of his tears at the corners of his mouth.

A horse-drawn cart went past. From a distance, only the lantern had been visible; close up, he discovered two people, a man and a woman, huddled against each other under a thick cover. He imagined he could feel the warmth of the two bodies pressed together, thigh to thigh.

"There's nothing to it, right?"

What did it matter if he'd had the sixty francs for the suit or not! He found the Seine at last, not far from a railroad bridge. He figured he must have come almost two miles.

Once again his watch had stopped. It was a terrible watch, but so what?

To think that he still didn't know exactly what "paranoiac" meant!

It was cold—more of his lousy luck! The river bank was covered with some kind of scratchy evergreen undergrowth, but he sat down to take off his shoes, which were from Groningen, and his socks, which his wife would be sure to recognize. Then he took off his coat, jacket, and pants. He shivered in the cold.

He'd bought his shirt in Paris; it was the one thing that was safe for him to keep on. But he felt ridiculous in it, so he took it off too.

Then he put his overcoat back on. For a long moment he sat quite still, looking at the flowing water just a few yards in front of him.

It really was cold, especially since his bare feet were in a puddle. The thing had to be done; best to do it fast. He blundered down to the water and threw his clothes in.

Then, lips quivering, he climbed back up to the top of the railway embankment. He reached the tracks. A green light shone, but it meant nothing to him. Then something extraordinary happened.

Till then, he'd been driven by a kind of fever within; now, suddenly, he grew calm. He'd never felt so calm in his life.

At the same time he looked around and wondered what he was doing there, stark naked under a blue overcoat, balancing on the ties so as not to bruise the soles of his feet on the gravel bed of the train track.

His face and hair were wet. He was shivering. He stared with stupefaction at the river that was bearing away the well-made clothes that had once belonged to him, to Kees Popinga!

To him, who had owned a house in the best neighborhood in Groningen and a new-model stove of the highest quality. Cigars on the mantelpiece! A radio costing four thousand francs!

If home hadn't been so far away, perhaps he could have tried going back. Maybe he could have snuck in through the kitchen window without anybody hearing. "There's nothing to it, right?"

What had he done, really? He'd wanted to . . .

No! He had to stop thinking. He couldn't allow himself to think about things like that, no matter what. The letter was sent.

Too bad! It was over! He'd already missed one train, on one of the tracks, and he couldn't afford to miss another. Not to mention that he might be discovered by one of the railway workers. He'd seen them out walking the tracks with their lanterns.

It was stupid, but so what? There was nothing he could do about it. It was stupid, but he lay across the track and rested his cheek on the rail.

The metal was ice cold and Popinga began to cry quietly. He searched the darkness. After a while a pinprick of light appeared.

After, there would be no more Popinga. No one would ever know, since there wouldn't be a head even. And because of his letter everyone would suppose . . .

He came close to jumping up: he'd heard the panting of the train; it was too cold. He could feel the train approaching the bend . . .

He'd told himself that he'd close his eyes. Yet the train appeared and he kept them open. He pulled up his legs, wide-eyed, openmouthed, unable to breathe.

The light came nearer. The noise was deafening, louder than

anything he'd ever heard, so loud that he thought he might already be dead.

Then he heard two voices, and then he heard nothing at all—which was when he realized that the train had come to a stop on another track. Two men were climbing out of the engine. Passengers were lowering their windows.

He stood up. He didn't know how. He didn't know how he managed to run either. He heard one of the men calling after him loudly: "Watch it! He's getting away!"

It wasn't true. He couldn't make it any farther. He threw himself down behind a bush. People were trampling around everywhere, and suddenly someone leapt on top of him, as if he were a kind of dangerous beast. His wrists were twisted back.

"Watch out! It's steep going down . . ."

It was all over for him. He didn't notice the express train finally passing on the track that he'd picked out, much less that they'd carried him into a second-class compartment, in the company of a man and a woman and the chief of the train's crew.

Too bad for them! It had nothing to do with him anymore!

12

On how dropping a chess piece into a cup of tea isn't the same as dropping it into a glass of beer.

TOO BAD for them! As for him, he didn't flinch. Wrapped in his overcoat, he walked down the platform at the Gare de l'Est. People were lined up on either side, joking around and pushing forward to see.

He maintained his dignity; he showed himself indifferent to their base curiosity, and in the stationmaster's office, he kept his calm too. He refused to answer any questions. He was happy to stare blankly at his interlocutors, treating them like so many half-unexpected objects.

From the moment that it was obvious, once and for all, that they would never understand!

He was given a narrow, hard sofa to sleep on. Then they woke him up and handed him a conductor's uniform. It was too tight and he couldn't button the jacket. That was perfectly fine by him.

Close to daybreak they brought him a pair of slippers. There were no shoes in his size.

It was the others who were disconcerted. They looked at him warily, but with a sort of respect, as if he had the power to cast a spell on them.

"You absolutely refuse to say who you are?"

No! It wasn't worth the trouble. He just shrugged.

They bundled him into a taxi. They drove into a courtyard, which he recognized as the courthouse. Then he was in a cell, bright enough and with a bed. Later, after he'd slept again, a small excitable man with a neatly trimmed gray beard came and poked at him, while asking endless questions.

Popinga didn't answer. But he hadn't yet made his discovery. That came when someone called out in the hall, "Dr. Abram! Phone call for Dr. Abram!"

Carefully locking the door behind him, the man went to respond to the call. So this was the only begetter of "paranoiac"!

What did it matter to Popinga if he was being held under special circumstances or not? All he wanted was a bit of peace. He felt like he could sleep for two days straight, three, even four, on a bench, on the floor, wherever.

From the moment that it was over...

He no longer had a watch; he no longer had anything. He was given warm milk to drink. He went back to bed and waited for the doctor to return. It must have been awhile, because he fell asleep, and it wasn't Abram who woke him, but somebody in street clothes. He was handcuffed and led off through a labyrinth of corridors and staircases to an office reeking of pipe smoke.

"You can leave us now."

Through the window you could see the murky yellow waters of the Seine flowing by. A man, nothing distinctive about him, a bit heavy, balding, was seated in the room. He motioned to Popinga to take a chair as well.

And Popinga meekly obeyed. Without any sign of impatience, he permitted himself to be examined and prodded.

"Yes," his interlocutor grunted. He'd checked him out from a distance and from up close. He'd looked into his eyes.

And suddenly he said, "Whatever were you thinking, Mr. Popinga?"

Kees didn't flinch. It didn't matter to him whether or not this was the famous Commissioner Lucas. And it didn't matter to him either when the door opened and a woman in a squirrel-fur coat walked in. She stopped in her tracks and said, "Yes, that's him. But how much he's changed!"

And after that? Whose turn next?

They went about their business in front of him, not in the least discomfited. Lucas was preparing a statement, which Jeanne Rozier signed, with an anxious glance at Popinga.

And after that? Would Louis, Goin, all the others, even Rose, come filing in?

If only they would leave him to sleep! What difference did it make to them, since they could come look at him and poke at him whenever they wished?

They left him alone, after which some more people came in, only to leave him alone again. Then they took him back to his cell. At last he could lie down.

Did they think he was so stupid that, now, he was going to tell them he wasn't crazy?

From the moment that the final hand was played...

Perhaps they could have avoided dragging him, day after day, to Commissioner Lucas's office—up and down every hall and stairway of the police station. Somebody would be standing in shadow.

"Recognize him?"

"No. It's not him. He wasn't so big."

He was shown his own letters.

"Is this your handwriting?"

"How should I know," he'd mumble in reply.

They could have brought him clothes that were the right size. They could have brought him some socks. He still didn't have any. And the people who hauled him off to be photographed and fingerprinted, taking him to a strange space at the very top of the building—they could have done a lot better than to leave him waiting in some anteroom, stark naked, for fifteen minutes or more.

And then, not long after...

Popinga had grown so resigned to whatever happened that when the day of the lecture arrived he didn't flinch. He hadn't expected it, though. They hadn't given him any warning. He was taken to a small room in which there were several people waiting—all obviously crazy. From time to time—every fifteen minutes or so—somebody came to fetch one of them. They didn't return. One after another!

Popinga was the last to go. Finally they came for him, too. He found himself standing on a dais in front of a blackboard. Tiny Dr. Abram was also there, in a state of elation. The room was poorly lit and at the foot of the dais thirty or so people sat taking notes—students, plus some others who seemed a little old for that.

"Please step forward. Don't be frightened. I'll be putting a few questions to you and I want you to answer in your own words."

Kees wasn't about to answer. He wasn't even going to listen! He heard the professor talking, using words much more complicated than "paranoiac." The students scribbled away furiously. A few of them came up to take a closer look. One had an instrument of some kind with which he took measurements of Kees's skull.

And after that? In any event, it was they who were the idiots! What more was there to say?

Another bright idea had been to bring him up to the visiting room; suddenly, through a grill they had confronted him with Mother. She'd thought it appropriate to dress in black, like a widow.

"Kees!" she exclaimed, wringing her hands. "Kees! Do you recognize me?"

He looked at her quite calmly, which must have been the reason she fainted with a cry.

What more would they come up with? Tell the whole story to the papers? So what? He didn't read them!

Other people came to see him—psychiatrists no doubt. Eventually he came to recognize them. Their questions never changed.

And he'd discovered a little trick of his. He'd look them square in the eye, as if amazed to see them making such a fuss, and it wasn't long before they threw up their hands.

To sleep! To eat! To sleep again! To dream of things that weren't exactly proper but quite agreeable most of the time.

One day they brought him a new suit. Mother must have had something to do with it, since it was almost the right size. The next day they put him in a police van. It pulled up in front of a train station. Two plainclothes cops took a seat with him on the train.

They seemed nervous. Kees, to the contrary, was delighted by the change of scenery. The blinds on the door to the compartment had been shut, but through the gaps he could see people moving around in the corridor. They were all trying to get a glimpse of him.

"Do you think we'll be back home by tonight?"

"Don't know. Depends on who picks him up."

After a while the two played cards. They gave him cigarettes. Clumsily, they stuck one between his lips, as if he couldn't manage it himself.

Everyone must have known who he was from the papers. Not that he really cared.

When they crossed the Belgian and the Dutch borders, he even smiled. One word from those fellows was enough to fend off the customs agents.

After the Dutch border, a policeman came in. He didn't speak French, so he sat in the corner reading the paper.

After that there was a great deal of coming and going and, at the train station, even photographers lying in wait. Once at the Amsterdam police station, Popinga didn't lose his composure. He smiled all the time or, when questioned, responded, "I don't know."

There was also a Dutch Dr. Abram, much younger than the one in Paris, who spent an hour or so taking Kees's blood, X-raying him, and listening to his chest, all the while maintaining a constant chatter. Popinga had to struggle not to laugh.

After which it must have all been over. People in the world outside must have been apprised, but not him. They must have decided he really was insane, since he wasn't assigned a lawyer and there was no mention of court.

Instead, he was sent to a large brick building on the outskirts of Amsterdam. Through the barred windows, he saw a field where people came to play soccer on Tuesdays and Sundays.

The food was good. He was allowed to sleep almost as much as he wanted. When it was time for exercise, he did his best.

He was alone in a little white room that was barely furnished. The most annoying thing was having to eat everything with a spoon. He wasn't permitted a knife or a fork.

But so what? In fact it was funny! They all considered him crazy!

Not so funny, however, were the cries that rang out at night from some of the other rooms. Muffled sounds would follow. He never made any noise himself. He wasn't that stupid.

The doctor was about his age. He too had a gray suit and wore gold-framed glasses. He came once a day, all plump and jolly.

"So, did you sleep well? Still in the dumps? You'll get over it!

You're in great health. You'll get over it any day now! Let's take your pulse..."

Popinga willingly extended his hand.

"That's perfect. Perfect! Still a little uncooperative, but that's sure to pass. I've seen cases..."

Eventually, in the visiting room with an orderly present, there was an encounter with Mrs. Popinga. She hadn't been able to talk in Paris. She'd burst into tears and fainted. This time she must have been prepared.

She had on the dress she wore when she volunteered at church—somber and black with a high neckline.

"Can you hear me, Kees? May I talk to you?"

He nodded yes—out of pity, perhaps for another reason.

"I am only allowed to see you the first Tuesday of every month... First, tell me, is there anything you need?"

He shook his head no.

"You're very unhappy, aren't you? So are we. I don't know if you know, if you can begin to imagine everything that's happened... First I had to move to Amsterdam where I found a job at the Jonghe cookie factory. I don't earn much, but they think a lot of me..."

He suppressed a smile—the Jonghe cookie factory, he recalled, had produced the pictures that his wife had loved to paste into her albums.

"I took Frida out of school. She didn't even cry. Now she's studying stenography, and Jonghe is going to hire her when she gets her diploma. You're not saying anything, Kees."

"I think that's just fine."

When she heard his voice she began to cry. She sobbed quietly, dabbing at her nose with her handkerchief.

"As for Carl, I don't know what to do; he wants to study navigation in Delfzijl. Maybe I can get him a scholarship."

So everything was working out! On the first Tuesday of

every month, she came. She never spoke about the past. She'd say, "Carl got the scholarship thanks to your old friend de Greef. He was very nice..."

Or: "We've moved again. That last place was just too expensive. We're with a very respectable woman. She's the widow of an officer, and she had an extra room and..."

Perfect, right? He slept a lot. He exercised and walked in the yard. The doctor, whose name he didn't know, took an interest in him.

"Is there anything you'd like?" he asked one day.

"A notebook and a pencil," Popinga replied. Though it was still too soon.

Yes, still too soon. The proof was his writing on the cover of the notebook, in self-consciously solemn letters, "The Truth About the Kees Popinga Case."

He had a lot of ideas on the subject. He promised himself to fill up the notebook and ask for others. He wanted to leave behind a true and accurate account of his case.

He'd had plenty of time to think about it. But on the first day, he only doodled around the title, arabesques in the style of the Romantic era. Then he slid the notebook under his mattress. The next day he looked at it for a long time before putting it away again.

He didn't have a calendar in his room. The only way he could keep track of time was through the first Tuesday of every month.

"What do you think, Kees? Frida's been offered a job with a journalist. I wonder if..."

Of course she wondered! He wondered, too... but why not?

"She should take it."

"Really?"

Wasn't it funny that they came to consult with him in the insane asylum? They were accustomed to asking his opinion about everything, even trivial things of the sort that, back in Groningen, the family had often discussed for hours.

"Sometimes I think that if we had an apartment with a kitchen...Obviously the rent would go up, but on the other hand..."

Of course, of course! He entirely approved. He put in his two bits. And Mother was more Mother than ever, though instead of sticking pictures from Jonghe's into an album at home, she was stuck working for Jonghe, doing God knows what.

"They give me half price on cookies."

"Isn't that wonderful!"

And wasn't everything just fine as it was? From the moment that it was clear that no one would ever understand...

He was so well behaved that they let him visit with two other inmates for several hours. One of them only lost it after dark and the other was the most reasonable man in the world so long as nobody contradicted him.

"Careful, Kees!" the doctor said. "No funny stuff, or it's back to solitary."

Why would he have picked a bone with either of those two poor men? He let them speak and, after they'd had their say, he was sure to start in, "When I was in Paris, I..."

But he quickly interrupted himself: "You'd never understand! In any case it doesn't matter. If only you knew how to play chess."

He tore some pieces from his notebook and made a board and pieces with which to play against himself. Not because he was bored—he never felt bored—but out of a sort of sentimental attachment to the past.

What difference did it make now? Even the thought of Commissioner Lucas left him unmoved. Once again he saw him circling around, interrogating him, prodding him, and he knew that he, Popinga, had won the game. And so?

No! He was no longer the type to pick a bone with his companions, or with Mother, who hadn't changed in the least, or with anyone. In the end he no longer even noticed the passage of time. One day Mother announced, "I really don't know what to say or do... The Jonghes' nephew is in love with Frida, and..." And he just smiled.

From the show of emotion she made he knew she was from the outside. She didn't have Kees Popinga's long experience. She was making much too much of the whole business. You'd have thought the fate of the world was at stake.

"What's he like?"

"Not bad... He's a fine young man... Maybe not in perfect health... He spent part of his childhood in Switzerland."

It was hilarious! How else to describe it?

"Is Frida in love?"

"She told me that if she didn't marry him she'd never marry at all."

The famous Frida—with her eyes that were completely empty of expression! Life still had its little surprises.

"Tell them to get married."

"It's just that the young man's parents..."

Yes, needless to say, they were a little hesitant about marrying their son off to the daughter of a lunatic.

Let them handle it! He couldn't do anything more. As it was, he was starting to push it, so much so that one day, when he was pondering a chess problem, the doctor watched over his shoulder for some fifteen minutes, waiting to see the solution. "Would you like to play a game sometimes, maybe at tea? I can see you're good."

"There's nothing to it, you know?"

But when he found himself face-to-face with the doctor, playing an actual game with actual black-and-white wooden pieces, he couldn't resist a little joke.

They weren't at the club in Groningen. They weren't on the boulevard Saint-Michel in Paris. On the table there were only cups of tea. And yet Popinga couldn't help it. He'd seen a threat from one of the doctor's bishops, and, as he made his own move, he palmed the piece, which he then dropped into his tea—just as he'd once done with the dark beer.

The doctor was thrown for an instant. Then he saw the piece floating around in the cup. He stood up, wiping his forehead. "I'm so sorry," he muttered. "I forgot that I have a meeting..."

For heaven's sake! What if Popinga had done it on purpose?! Just because he took a certain pleasure in revisiting the past...

"No, no, I'm the one who's sorry," he said. "It's an old story—hard to explain. You wouldn't understand, anyway."

Too bad! Anyway, it was safer like this. He knew because the doctor had had the idea of asking to see the notebook he'd given him to record his memoirs. There was nothing to read beyond THE TRUTH ABOUT THE KEES POPINGA CASE.

The doctor looked up, puzzled, as if wondering why his patient hadn't written at greater length. And Popinga, with a tight smile, felt constrained to murmur, "There isn't any truth, you know?"

TITLES IN SERIES